A Stag Family Christmas

Stag Brothers

Book 4

Lainey Davis

A Stag Family Christmas

 Created with Vellum

About This Book

The weather outside is frightful this Christmas, and the heat is on for the Stag Brothers. Caramel sauce isn't the only sticky mess for these broody brothers, who each face challenges in love and life.

Timber Stag led his family and his law empire with the same stern hand until Alice stumbled into his life. Just when he learns to relax and enjoy the cocoa, everything unravels. Tim's right-hand woman, his sister-in-law Juniper, opts to leave Stag Law, and each of Tim's brothers skates on thin ice at home. Tim needs a Christmas miracle to help put everyone back together again.

Thatcher Stag had worked his way off the naughty list and settled down with Emma, but when a health scare rocks Emma to her core, Thatcher needs help navigating the fog.

Meanwhile, Tyrion Stag seems to be on Santa's nice list. He's got the perfect wife, a stellar pro hockey career...but the thrill of the road seems to have lost its luster. Ty feels torn when hockey pulls him from his family, and he needs a star to guide him this Christmas.

This rollicking adventure follows our favorite family through a holiday season bursting with action. Emotions run high, the pressure cooker is on, and a snowy Christmas Eve changes the Stag family forever.

A Stag Family Christmas picks up where the previous books left off, with all the steamy passion you've come to love, but can still stand alone for new readers. Jump into the fast-pace series readers are calling a delightful, intriguing roller coaster that's equal parts funny, sweet and heart wrenching. Don't worry—all Lainey Davis lovers get their Happily Ever After eventually!

Content Note

I hope it's not too much of a spoiler to tell you this book features pregnancy.

At the time I wrote this book, Americans like these characters had a choice whether to continue their pregnancy. Effective June 24, 2022, Americans no longer have that choice. If I were writing this book today, the plot and emotions expressed would be different. The stakes would be different. These characters would have had a different journey, and I think this trope carries new weight. Because our right to bodily autonomy has been revoked, I know reading this story might be difficult for some. Please know that I am fighting for reproductive justice.

Chapter 1

Thatcher

I hate when the phone rings while I'm blowing glass. It messes up my concentration. In my haste to answer and set down my work, I drop my damn cell phone. But my assistant, Cody, is bellowing so loud I can hear him anyway. "Dude, you better get over here," he shouts.

"Where the hell *are* you, Code?" I wipe my hands on my jeans and pick up the phone so I can hear him better. I switch off the radio, too. They're already playing Christmas music. In late October! "What's that, Cody?"

"I'm in the fucking tattoo shop, like I said, and I mean it. You'd better get here. Stat." I sigh and look at my watch. It's three. If I leave my studio now, for whatever the hell Cody needs, I wont' be able to get back into my creative zone before Emma gets home from work. Before we lived together, I'd just work all night long if I had inspiration. What the hell did I care? But now I actually enjoy spending time outside of my glass studio. My girl has taught me a lot about loving life, and usually it shows up in my art. I've been busy enough to bring Cody on full-time.

Emma hates how much I've been working lately, but I've got orders out the ass from people wanting Christmas gifts and private lessons and all that shit I hate about the business side of Stag Glass. I really can't swing an impromptu trip to the tattoo parlor. "I don't know, Cody. I'm working here."

About a year ago, one of the top architects in Pittsburgh commissioned me to create a custom piece of glass for his new bar, and to make all the damn glassware he'd need to serve drinks. Ever since then, people are beating down my door for highballs and shot glasses, and wanting date-night glass-blowing classes where I serve wine. I keep telling my agent I'm not an Ikea. She keeps smiling and handing me contracts.

"Thatcher, I swear to god, you need to see this." Cody hangs up on me.

"Motherfucker," I growl, shutting the furnace and flicking off the lights. I'll have to come back to work after Emma goes to bed. I rub my hands through my hair while I wait for my truck to warm up. It's been abnormally cold this fall, and the engine sputters a bit in my beat up old Ranger. *Better than walking*, I think, shifting into gear and heading toward my old neighborhood.

I plan to spend as little time as possible dealing with Cody's crisis so I can get back in time to give Emma a ride home from work. She can't drive because of her epilepsy, even though she's been seizure-free for a long time. I used to live in an old industrial neighborhood that wasn't walking distance to anywhere. Relocating close to Emma was the last I could do, considering she walks *everywhere,* all the time.

I don't think she took enough layers along today to walk home in subfreezing wind gusts. I shoot Emma a text that I'll be waiting for her in the parking lot when she gets done with her meeting, and then I open the door to see what kind of trouble is brewing at Green Mamba

Tattoo. I figure Cody changed his mind halfway through a neck tattoo or something. I've had my fair share of ink regret. Green Mamba is pretty good at transforming mistakes into mystique.

Cody meets me inside, where I raise an eyebrow at him and he yanks me behind the privacy curtain. "Thatcher. Look." He points, and I see my brothers' wives giggling, leaning over a binder of designs. And then, holy shit. There's *my* girl. Emma Cheswick, my previously untattooed girlfriend, stands right with them.

"What the hell is going on here, Chezz?" I bark out. "I thought you had a meeting." Hearing my voice, she whips her red head around and drops her jaw. Juniper and Alice peek over her shoulder, register my presence, and then look at each other and laugh.

Emma coughs. "Well," she says, blushing. "I'm *meeting* the girls here. They're getting the Stag family tattoo." Years ago, I designed a tattoo and my brothers and I all came here to get it on my eighteenth birthday. The tattoo is a silhouette of a stag leaping over mountain laurel, in honor of our mother, Laurel Stag. Mom died in a car crash when we were kids, and we've all got the tattoo on our chest, above our heart.

For me, it was the first of many, many tats. I'm not so sure how Ty and Tim will feel about *their* wives getting the family ink, but the idea of my girl doing it turns me the hell on.

"Are you getting it, too?" I step forward and grasp Emma's hand, my voice quiet. The idea of her laying a permanent claim to me, right on her skin...shit. I rub her palm with my thumb, imagining her milk-white skin in contrast to the black ink.

Emma shakes her head, her eyes sad. "I'd want to talk to Dr. Khalsa about it first," she says. Emma's neurologist is a top-notch researcher and has helped her keep all her symptoms in check. She hasn't had a seizure since we first met. She points a thumb at Alice, Tim's wife, who has now hopped up on the table and removed her sweater. "The girls just asked me to come along while *they* got inked," Emma says. She frowns at me. "It's supposed to be Stag-women only, but Cody wandered in and spilled the beans."

Emma tilts her head to the side and makes a sexy, pouty face at me. "You wouldn't call your brothers and spoil the surprise, would you, Thatchy?"

I roll my eyes at her. "Jesus, Emma. Do not call me Thatchy ever again." She laughs. I look at the transfer the artist is about to stick on Alice, and furrow my brow. "That's not my design."

Alice beams, and sucks in her breath as the alcohol wipe hits her shoulder blade. She pulls her tank top to the side a bit to give more access and tells me that she asked the artist to make some tweaks. I squint a little closer and see Alice added a baby deer curled up next to its father. "I added Petey," she says, smiling when she says my nephew's name. "There's plenty of space for more little fawns, too."

I draw Emma in for a kiss, appreciating how much my family all supports each other. These women don't *have* to love us, but they're here for us. And for each other, apparently.

This connection and warmth is so different from what we grew up with. After our mother died, our father was drowning in grief and depression. He turned to booze, and walked out on us, leaving teenaged Timber to raise me and Tyrion. It's taken Alice years to soften Tim up around the edges, and I love her twist on the tattoo. "I think you're a bad-ass mama Stag, Alice," I say, patting her leg. She winces as the needle starts to vibrate, but she grits her teeth and smiles at me. "Emma, you sticking around?"

She nods as Juniper clings to her arm. "I've got to talk this one out of leaving," Emma says. "Honestly, I don't know how someone could train hard enough to win an Olympic medal at rowing, but feel scared of a tiny little needle."

Juniper glares at Emma. "You don't get to make these comparisons until you're facing that giant needle gun yourself, madam!"

I make eyes with the tattoo artist—he's done at least six of my tats—and wink. "Listen, Em, how about I go for a walk and leave you to your *meeting*. I'll be back in fifteen minutes, and I'm sure both Juniper and Alice will be long done by then. Want me to bring you anything?"

She grins and asks me to pick something at the bakery to surprise her. I wish I'd thought to offer that. I kiss her forehead and fist-bump Cody on my way out. Turns out he's still fully committed to his neck tattoo.

* * *

I decide to get a box of macarons for everyone, wondering again why I hadn't thought to offer. My brothers seem to fall into family life so naturally. Once they fell for their women, that was it. They were all in. I always need to be reminded how to open up to Emma, trust her. Moving in with her was a big gesture for me. Knowing she didn't get the tattoo today makes me worry it wasn't enough.

Alice and Juniper are fully clothed and inked when I deliver the treats. Emma seems a little off, so I usher her out to the truck. "Ready to go home, babe?" She shakes her head.

"Can you take me back to work? I want to push through something I'm revising."

"You sure? It's really fucking cold out there. Why not write from home and let me warm you up?" I'm still worked up at the mental image of Emma getting a tattoo, and, frankly, I can't wait to get close to her skin, inky or not.

I slide a hand up her thigh, but feel her stiffen. *Hmm, not good.* I withdraw my hand and look at her. "What's wrong?"

She huffs. *Shit. What did I do?* "You asked me if I'm getting the STAG FAMILY tattoo. But I'm not a Stag, am I, Thatcher?"

"Of course you are, Chezz. What are you talking about?"

She shakes her head. "I'm not. I'm not a Stag. I'm your live-in girlfriend."

"Shit, Emma. You know you mean everything to me. I'm trying really hard here."

She rolls her eyes. "I think I'm convenient for you, is what I am."

"How can you say that? I moved my whole studio so I could be with you. So I could be supportive of your job."

"Am I supposed to be grateful of your sacrifice?" Her eyes flare and she looks really angry.

I rake my fingers through my long hair again. I guess my suspicions were right, but I didn't know Emma was this upset about the direction of our relationship. "I want to make a life with you, Emma. I *want* you to want the Stag family tattoo."

Emma starts crying then, and I know things are worse than I thought. "Why didn't you talk to me before you were this upset?"

"I didn't know I was this upset until everyone else was getting the Stag brand and I felt left out."

"Should I go back and ask Jason to ink you up real quick?" Emma snorts at that suggestion. I seize upon this tiny gesture and press on. "Or do you want me to tattoo your name on my ass? I would, you know, Chezz."

I slam the truck into first gear outside our building and yank on the e-brake. I look over at Emma, ready to keep hashing this out, but she's gone gray and clammy. "Emma?" She reaches out a hand and squeezes my arm, but her body goes stiff and her muscles begin to twitch. "Emma!"

She's having a seizure. *Shit, shit, shit.* I can't remember what to do. It's been awhile since we talked through this possibility.

Her body slumps over and stills. I unbuckle my seat belt and grab her phone from her coat pocket. Unlocking it, I dial up her neurologist and try to suppress my panic.

Chapter 2
Ty

Coach blows the whistle and we all sink to the ice, exhausted. He's been riding us so hard this season. We haven't won the Cup since the first year I was on the Fury, but we got to the semifinals last year. Coach can smell the silver polish on that big-ass bowl, and so can every guy out here. But fuck, I'm tired. "That's it for today, men," he bellows. "You know what I'm asking Santa for this year, and you're the little elves who're gonna bring it to me." I don't even have the energy left to cuss at him.

I pull myself up and limp to the locker room. I can't wait to get home, so I skip the showers. I want to yank my wife into the tub with me and wrap her long legs around my ribs until they don't hurt anymore. I almost fumble the keys, I'm so eager to get inside, but when I get home, our place is dark and quiet. *Shit.* Did I forget? I swear Juniper was going to be home after I got out from practice this week.

My wife was a partner in my brother's law firm, but now she's running for judge. I'm proud as fuck that she's trying to get elected, but between my pro hockey schedule and her campaign events, I hardly see her. I flick on the lights and see a note in the kitchen.

> Ran into the office to wrap up a case file.
> Be home by 9. I'm sorry!!! —JJ

Fuck. I'm sweaty and horny and my wife is at work. I grab a peach from the counter, but as I'm eating it, all I can think about is tonguing Juniper. I nestle into the couch and call her up on video chat.

"Ty! I'm so sorry!" She seems flustered. Her hair is a bit of a mess and I see her wince as she leans to grab a file. "How was practice?"

"Coach is trying to kill us."

She scoffs, still not looking up, and says, "Or maybe you let yourself get soft, easing up on conditioning in the off-season." I fucking love it when Juniper challenges me. She won a damn Olympic gold medal in rowing and she's fit as fuck. We train together whenever we can and living with another athlete makes it so much easier for me to stick with my training and my diet. I toss the peach aside, though, because I don't want health food right now.

I love looking at my wife in work mode, wearing her power suit. I reach into the waist of my mesh shorts and give my dick a tug. She looks up briefly and squints, looking at our condo. "We need to talk about getting the housekeeper to come more often."

Juniper starts talking about how shit is falling apart at home—she's right. We have laundry everywhere—but I mostly stare at her lips and stroke myself a little harder. "Babe, angle the monitor down a bit."

She raises an eyebrow. "What are you talking about?"

I grunt.

"Ty, are you jerking off right now?" She can holler at me all she wants if she's going to pull her shoulders back like that. Her tits are centered in the screen of my phone, moving up and down a little as she starts yelling at me. But then she tilts the screen so I can see her face.

"I wanted to fuck you so bad after practice, Junebug." She licks her lips. "Take off your suit jacket and let me see your blouse."

Juniper looks over her shoulder. She stands up and walks off screen, and I hear her closing her office door. Hell yeah! It's on.

She walks back over to her desk and leans forward. The laptop camera is lined up with the neck of her blouse and I can see her bra a little bit as she says, "You're telling me you're so fucking horny you couldn't wait a few more hours for this?"

I groan, imagining how good it feels when she lets me slide my cock in between her tits. "Fuck, Juniper. I need you so much." She disappears from the screen and I sit up, but I start stroking again when I see that she's settled back in her desk chair with her legs spread open. She hikes up her pencil skirt slowly, teasing me, and I start sweating when I catch a glimpse of her silk panties.

"What would you do to these if you were here right now, Ty?" She drums her fingers on her thighs and I want to dive through the screen and push her hand aside.

"I'd bury my face right in your beautiful pussy, baby. I'd lick you until you scream my name." I grunt, feeling the build up of pleasure as I fist my own cock, remembering how good it feels to make my wife come with my tongue.

Juniper's fingers are flying around her clit now. I can see the shine of her wedding ring catch the light as she moves her hand around. *She's mine,* I think, picking up speed. "Tell me more, Ty," she pants, dropping one hand to rub her nipple as she keeps strumming her needy bud.

"Oh, god, baby, I want to sink inside you. I want to bury my cock to the root and wrap those long legs of yours around my back. I want to move with you until we both forget our names. Fuck!" I'm so close.

"Ooooooh, yes, Tyrion. I love it when you fuck me. Shit, Ty. Yes!" She pants and her hand stops.

"I just came, babe. Are you close?" She leans forward again and I can see a fine sheen of sweat on her skin. Her face is flushed with pleasure and she's breathing heavy. "I want to see, Ty. I want to see you come."

Who could say no to that? "Aahhh!" I shout as I come, white hot spunk spraying my fist. I'm gasping for breath. I slump back in the chair, waiting for my eyes to roll back into their sockets properly. "Juniper, you blow my mind, baby. I love you so much."

I see an incoming call from my brother Thatcher, but I click decline. I'm busy with my wife here.

Juniper smiles and tucks her loose hair behind her ear. She straightens up in her chair, winces again, and starts to gather up her files. *What's with the wincing*, I wonder, tucking my junk back in my shorts. "I love you, too, babe. How about you let me get back to this and we can go for it in person in a few hours?" How can she just shift gears so quickly? That's what I love about her— Juniper is just good at everything.

Thatcher calls again. Jesus, will nobody let me talk to my damn wife? "Junebug," I sigh. "I gotta go. Thatcher keeps calling. Hurry home to me?"

She nods, but I can see she's already back in her work. She's trying to wrap everything up there at the firm. I know she's trying not to get too confident, but Juniper is going to win this election. Everyone can see it. I hang up and decide to finally shower before I call my brother back. I'm even more of a mess than I was right after practice.

I think about how I can clean this place up a little bit before Juniper gets home—there's a 24-hour dry cleaner not too far away and I can at least drop off all our laundry—and, brother forgotten, I climb into a steaming shower with a plan.

Chapter 3
Tim

The office is too quiet today. My wife packed up our son from the on-site daycare and took him home a few hours earlier. Said she had some outside business to attend to, whatever that means. I frown in the direction of my office door, thinking about how a few years ago, I hated any form of disruption here at work. This place was cutthroat, but ever since Alice and Juniper came along, our culture has changed as much as our client base. Hell, I just signed a damn approval for a holiday party at the indoor trampoline park.

Juniper's idea, of course. Right before she leaves us for the judge's robes. I should be happier for her. Our profits have increased and we all seem to enjoy our jobs a little more. This is why we need her. I'm thrilled for Juniper as my sister-in-law. She's going to kick ass in this election and make a fair judge. I'm damn proud to have her in the family.

But as her boss? I'm going to be screwed. I'm losing an amazing lawyer. She's helped me diversify and build my empire here at Stag Law. At least I still have my wife working here, keeping me sane. And fed. My stomach rumbles and I realize I missed lunch today. If Alice had been here, she would have come and found me. Made sure I tasted whatever she was making.

I hired her as the corporate chef here at Stag Law, but I had no idea she would transform my entire life. I used to think I only lusted after her, that once I slept with Alice she'd stop driving me to distraction. But actually, Alice taught me how to trust. How to let someone love me. Now, I can't think straight when she's not around.

I can count on one hand the number of times I've left work before five, but I'm not getting anything done here and I'm just making myself grouchy. I decide to go home and find Alice. I stop by my assistant's desk on my way out the door. Donna raises an eyebrow at me and says, "You don't have any outside meetings on your schedule today. What's up, Timber?"

"Donna," I say, rapping her desk. "I'm going home early today."

Her mouth hangs open for a second, and then she shakes her head and pulls herself together. "I'll have a briefing on your desk for your key cases and clients in the morning."

"Thanks, Donna." I pause. "You should go home early, too. I can do the briefing from home." She smiles and shakes her head at me as I take the elevator to the parking garage.

I realize Alice has left me without a car, so I call up a ride. This shit makes me nervous. I hate letting other people drive me around. My mother was killed in a car accident, and while Alice is helping me work on letting go of my tendency to control everyone, I'm pretty stuck on needing to control the steering wheel, especially with my family on board. I pull up my case notes on my phone to take my mind off the driver.

There's a note from Ty's agent—coach is concerned Ty has lost his edge. I wonder what's going on there. I think about calling him to take my mind off this ride, but we pull up to my house just as I finish reading my email.

I can see my front door is hanging open even though it's freezing outside. I also hear a ruckus in the house, so I know Alice's sister Amy is over with her three boys. I exhale deeply, wondering if they've shoved Petey down the laundry shoot again or flushed my best neck ties down the toilet.

My home life used to be a lot more orderly, too. I have to remind myself how miserable I was with my tidy corners and clean countertops. But shit, do all these kids have to leave the door hanging open?

I close the door behind me and try to yell out that I'm home early, but the boys are shrieking and running up and down the stairs. "Ouch!" Something hits me in the neck. I hear my nephews cackling and see that it's just a foam bullet from a toy gun. *Little snots*. I walk toward the kitchen rubbing my neck, and I freeze in my tracks when I see my wife.

Her back is toward me and she's holding her wild, curly hair to the side. Her sister Amy is leaning close to check out something on Alice's back. I can see the skin is red and raised. I walk closer as Amy meets my eye. She smiles and I peer down. My wife has a tattoo.

I touch the warm skin of the fresh tattoo and Alice yelps. She turns around in my arms and her huge, violet eyes look up into mine. "Damn it. It was supposed to be a surprise."

My wife got the Stag family tattoo on her shoulder blade. I'm speechless, touched. I just never considered that she'd want to be part of that with me and my brothers. "Alice," I breathe. "I'm definitely surprised. Can I see it again?"

She nods and turns around. When I see that she added a baby deer to the image, I am so overcome that I have to grab the counter to steady myself. Alice bites her lip and looks at me, eyes wide. "Tim, you have to say something. You're glowering."

"I'm...not glowering, Alice." I run my fingers through her hair. "I'm just so happy you did this."

"Really?" she asks, licking her lower lip now. Fuck, if she keeps doing that I'm going to have to go back outside and stand in the cold air until my dick calms down. "You like it, Mr. Stag?"

I nod and she extends up on tiptoes to give me a kiss. "Good," she says, picking up her sweater from the counter. "I was going to do this whole big thing and show you, make you dinner. Since when do you ever come home early?"

Petey zooms by in pursuit of his cousins, and I snatch him up into my arms. "It was too quiet at work," I say, nuzzling his curly hair with my nose.

Amy explains that her role in this plan was to take Petey over to her house until bedtime, and I raise my eyebrows as Amy whistles "Santa Baby" and starts gathering up the boys. Alice shoves a huge container of lasagna into Amy's arms and helps with the assembly line of coats and sneakers. They're gone in a whirlwind before I can even process Amy's mischievous wink. When I turn around, Alice has disappeared.

"Babe? Where'd you go?"

"Come and find me, Mr. Stag," she yells, and then she giggles. I loosen my tie as I climb up the stairs.

Our bedroom door is ajar. "Is my grandma home, or did you send her away, too—" My words catch in my throat when I see Alice fully nude, on hands and knees on our bed.

"Come here," she says, looking over her shoulder. Her wild curls fall over the tattoo and her round ass points up, begging me to massage it. So I do. "This is how you were supposed to find me," she says, "and then I was going to ask you to kiss my back." I comply, planting a row of kisses up and down her spine, just like she likes. Soft and gentle.

"Then what," I ask, licking a line down to the curve of her hip, peppering kisses along the silvery stretch marks from where her belly stretched growing Petey. I love tracing the fine lines on her body, the reminders that she grew our baby, forever altering our lives by making this beautiful combination of both of us. Her body changed forever to give me my son, and I fucking love that. I keep licking and kissing, massaging her ass just how she likes.

Alice moans softly in appreciation and tells me, "You were supposed to gather up my hair like you always do, and then you were supposed to notice my tattoo, and say, 'What have you done, Mrs. Stag?'"

Once I do as she asks, I can't control myself anymore. I'm so overcome. My dick is like steel, bursting to get out of my suit pants. I've got her mass of curls twisted in one fist and I hastily unfasten my pants with the other. My cock springs out, begging to be inside her. I reach down between my wife's legs and find her slick with wanting. She sighs as I massage her folds and I lean forward to kiss her shoulder where the skin is still slightly pink around the edges of the tattoo. I line myself up and thrust. When I ease inside her, I whisper into her ear, "You're mine, Alice Stag. And I'm yours."

I move slowly in and out, savoring the feel of her body. My hands are everywhere, massaging Alice's peachy skin while she practically purrs. I love making her feel good. I love how she takes me out of that anxious space in my head, keeps me present in the moment. Suddenly, I need to see her face, and I pull out, flipping her over. Alice squeaks and giggles and nuzzles my nose with hers as she wraps her short legs as far around me as she can. "Come back inside me, Tim," she says. "I need you."

I capture her mouth in a kiss and she reaches down to guide me back home. Our eyes meet and I can feel her pleasure building. I know I won't last much longer. This is too intense to draw out, but I have to get her there first. "Alice," I gasp. "Come for me, baby." She nods as I reach between us, rubbing her clit how I know she needs it. I increase my pressure and slow my rolling fingertips until I feel her start to pulse around me.

"Oh god, Tim! Fuck, yes. I'm coming!" Alice's hips roll into me, drawing me in deeper. I swell inside her and, locked in her violet gaze, I lose myself. I spill inside Alice and, just like the very first time, I am lost to her. Amazed at what she and I can do together.

"Alice, god, I need you so much," I say when I can talk again.

"I'm not going anywhere." She wraps her arms around me and kisses me until my heart slows.

* * *

A bit later, Alice gets up to take a shower and finish the special dinner she promised she was making me before Petey comes home. I hear her singing to herself as she moves through the house and I stretch back on the bed, arms behind my head. It's still so strange to me to feel content. For so many years, I held my breath. On edge, worried all the time about keeping my family safe. I still have a family to protect, but Alice is really helping me see that I don't have to do it all on my own.

I'm about to nod off when I hear my phone buzzing from somewhere. At one point, I had kicked off my pants and I look around the mess of blankets until I find it, Thatcher's face coming up on the screen. He usually doesn't call— Thatcher's more of a text guy. "What's up, brother?"

"Tim!" he gasps, sounding panicked. "I don't know what to do."

I sit up and start to get dressed, flying into action mode when I hear the concern in my brother's voice. "Okay, I'll help you. Thatch—what happened?"

"It's Emma," he gasps. "We're in the emergency room."

I'm walking to the car before he gets the sentence out. I mouth "Emma's in the hospital" to Alice, kissing her cheek. She clicks off the burner on the stove and pulls out her phone to call her sister.

"Hang on, Tim. I'm coming with you." As soon as she says it, I'm relieved. Alice always knows how to talk to Thatcher, reassure him. Together, we head to the hospital.

Chapter 4
Thatcher

Dr. Khalsa meets me in the emergency room after Emma's seizure. We know each other pretty well, since I usually drive Emma to and from her appointments. I leave my truck running in the parking lot and scoop Emma into my arms, stomping past the security guard. Dr. Khalsa grabs a wheelchair and tells the guard to please see to my truck while we walk back to a room.

"Did she mention an aura this morning?" He furrows his brow. She's out cold, either asleep or passed out. I don't even know. I shake my head as he hooks her up to some monitors. "She didn't mention any symptoms at all." Once he sighs seeing some numbers, I can see him relax a little and I know he's not worried anymore. "We were having a fight," I tell him. "She's angry with me. Would that have caused her to have a seizure?"

He frowns. "I really don't think she'd have a tonic clonic event with no warning signs over a domestic dispute," he says. He pulls out his tablet device and starts clicking around. "She hasn't had a seizure in several years now and hasn't even reported an aura since we began the medical cannabis trial."

His cheeks puff out as he exhales. "I'm going to run some bloodwork and see if maybe something else is going on that triggered the seizure." I see him studying something on Emma's chart and he pages a nurse. I pace around the room, tugging at my hair and trying not to panic, but I freeze in my tracks when I hear him say, "Standard panel...oh, and why don't we do a pregnancy screening. Let's rule that out first."

"Pregnancy?" My voice is louder than I intended, but what the hell? Emma's on the pill. I don't even know what it means if someone with epilepsy gets pregnant, but that sounds pretty scary to me, especially since she just had a major seizure.

Dr. Khalsa pats my arm. "I was just reading here that she was on an antibiotic this fall for a sinus infection. Antibiotics render birth control pills ineffective." He squints, studying my face. "Did you and Emma use protection during intercourse when she was taking that medication?"

I sink into a chair, unable to answer him. Emma and I have never used condoms. Ever. He clicks his tongue and follows the nurse out of the room. I hadn't even noticed her drawing vials of blood from Emma's arm. I look at Emma on the bed, red hair splayed everywhere, skin pale. She looks so small. God, I can't shake the feeling that this is my fault.

What the fuck was I thinking, not proposing to Emma? Not taking her to the courthouse to make things official? I let myself get used to her, just sort of comfortable with our lives. But of course she wants more. From my end, she's it for me. I'm not going anywhere without her. But I'm still learning how to be a decent guy. What if Emma gets sick of coaching me through all my baggage? *What the hell is wrong with me?*

I need my brothers or I'm going to freak the fuck out, but none of them are answering their damn phones. By the time I get Tim to pick up, I'm almost hyperventilating, but he tells me he will be here soon.

Dr. Khalsa comes back in the room and drags a chair next to me. "Thatcher," he says. "Emma still doesn't have you listed on her HIPAA forms. Are you legally married?"

My mouth hangs open. "No," I whisper. "But she's my world, Doc. You know that. I built a house for her. We live together and share a bank account. What are you saying here?"

He sighs through his nose. "I can't discuss the details of her health with anyone who isn't next of kin or listed on her privacy forms."

I feel my temper flaring, my panic starting to rise. "Well who the fuck does she have listed? Don't tell me it's still her fucking parents because—"

"Nicole Kennedy," he says. "Do you know her?"

Relief floods over me at the name of Emma's best friend. Nicole is like a female Tim. When they were college roommates, Nicole dragged

Emma to Dr. Khalsa, knowing with proper care she could control her seizures and live a normal life. Nicole has been there for Emma for years... but I'm her man. I'm the one here with her at these appointments now. Did Emma leave me off her forms to spite me because I haven't proposed to her yet?

I'm pissed and helpless here, but at least I don't have to deal with Emma's snooty mother and politician father. I nod to Dr. Khalsa and pull out my phone to call Nicole. As soon as I tell her Emma's in the hospital, I hear her screaming something at her assistant. Nicole works around the clock. I always wonder whether she and Tim were separated at birth. As I try to explain details, Nicole starts yelling and trying to micromanage *me*. She hangs up before I can give her more details, so I assume she's on her way.

Dr. Khalsa is still standing there, checking Emma out, and she's still totally zonked. He nods, reading some test results the nurse brings him, and I decide I'm not above begging. "Doc," I say to him. "Are you saying even if she's pregnant you can't tell me about that? About what it means?"

He shakes his head. The guy looks genuinely sorry, but I want to pull my hair out. "But it would be my baby," I tell him. "Mine and Emma's together." My voice cracks, and I know I'm going to lose it if somebody doesn't tell me what the hell is happening.

I start pacing the room in tight circles until I hear Nicole clomping down the hall in her high heels. "What's the situation here?" she doesn't even look at me, though, and strides directly to the doctor, saying, "Nicole Kennedy, in-case-of-emergency-person for Emma Cheswick, reporting for duty."

She gives him a salute gesture and Dr. Khalsa asks if she'd like me leave the room. I'm really glad I don't have to kill someone, because Nicole says, "Obviously not. Spill it, doc. Don't make me sorry I brought Emma to your clinic all those years ago."

Chapter 5

Ty

I must have fallen asleep on the couch waiting for Juniper. She wakes me up with a soft kiss, pulling the heating pad off my shoulder. I feel a rush of cold air and I groan, trying to figure out where I am and what happened. "Sshh," she whispers. "It's just me."

Other parts of my body wake up faster than my head, especially when she starts rubbing my arm and straddles my knee while she digs out the remote to turn off the TV. "Shit, Junebug. What time is it?"

"It's late," she says. "I'm really sorry, Ty. I wanted to get all that work sorted so I can focus on this last week of the campaign. We can spend time together tomorrow."

I shake my head and pull her onto my lap. "Nope," I say, running my fingers through her short, dark hair. It's sleek and smooth and I love how it flows against my skin. "The Fury leave for Denver tomorrow morning."

"Fuck," she says. She sits up and looks me in the eye. "Seriously? How could I lose track of your schedule like that?" She climbs off my lap and kicks the couch.

"It's okay, baby. Come back and sit on my lap again..."

"No," she shouts. "It's not okay! I signed you up to make an appearance with me tomorrow night. Fuck, I'll have to redo the whole plan for the event if you won't be there. Plus everyone will be watching hockey."

"I thought you just said we can hang out?"

"Yeah," she says. "At a fundraiser at someone's house. They're writing postcards and donating to the campaign. We were going to make an appearance..." She drifts off, noticing the table is clear. "Where the hell is all the laundry?"

I lean back with my hands crossed behind my head like some smug fucker. "I took it to the all-night cleaner, JJ. Your panties and my boxers are swirling around together as we speak." Realizing I took care of everything, Juniper groans. This is not the effect I was going for when I cleaned up our place. I can see in her face that she's overwhelmed. She sinks into a chair. "Hey, babe," I pat my lap. "I've got a comfortable seat for you right here."

She doesn't move, but starts mumbling about how she didn't think it would be this way. She says something about Thanksgiving, and I can tell she's spiraling, so I walk over to her and start massaging her temples. "Juniper Jones," I whisper into her ear. "I don't want you to worry about anything. Tell me what you need me to do."

She turns then and buries her face in my shirt, crying a little bit. "What's going to happen if I get elected," she asks. "You're gone half the time and then I'll be gone half the time and I don't even know where you put the laundry. Who is going to buy the bread for Thanksgiving?"

"Won't Alice bake the bread," I ask, trying to soothe her. But this just makes Juniper cry.

"I told her I'd get it," she sobs. "I wanted to feel like I could do this family dinner thing and still contribute *and* run a campaign *and* get the damn tattoo, but I didn't even remember to get cash for the housekeeper."

I bend down and lift her out of her seat. Juniper is a tall woman. She's five-ten, and an athlete, but I'm a professional hockey player. I bench press more than she weighs. I know she loves that I can haul her around like she's weightless. Okay, maybe not weightless, but damn if I'll ever let her hear me struggle to lift her. "What tattoo, babe," I ask, carrying her to our room. I like that she's tall enough to look me in the eye when we're dancing.

I place her on the edge of our bed and get to work removing her office wear. She winces again, and I furrow my brow. She looks up at me with those big, brown eyes of hers and I kneel on the ground in front of her as she peels off her blouse. She twists to the side a bit and then I see it. My wife got the same tattoo as me and my brothers.

"Woah," I say. She smiles shyly. "Babe, that's fucking amazing."

"Do you like it? I wanted to feel close to you, especially since I never changed my name."

I kiss her skin all around the tattoo, careful not to touch it directly. "I fucking love it," I tell her. "Now I need one for you." She laughs. "I'm serious. What should I get? I'll put your face on my other pec." I tip her back on the bed and she falls asleep plotting out potential designs I could get inked on my chest. I pull out my phone to search for some images, and I remember that I never called Thatcher back. *Shit,* I think, looking at the screen. I missed about five calls from each of my brothers.

It's past midnight, so I don't bother calling Tim. I wouldn't want to wake up Petey. But Tim picks up when I call Thatcher's phone. *That's weird,* I think. "Hey," Tim says. "We have a situation." I look over at Juniper and, not wanting to wake her, either, I step back into the living room.

"What happened? Why are you answering Thatcher's phone?"

"Emma's pregnant," he says, his voice unreadable, like he's already in lawyer mode.

"Woah! That's amazing! Another nephew for Team Stag. Obviously it'll be a boy. Fucking awesome," I start celebrating. This isn't like when Tim knocked up Alice after they were only together a few weeks. Emma's been with Thatcher for ages. "Will she have the baby at that midwife center where we were born? Where Alice had Petey?"

"Tyrion, Emma has epilepsy, remember?" And with that, Tim's words bring back the memory of how Emma had a big seizure at a family dinner once. She ended up in the hospital then, although she said that was mainly just a precaution.

"What does that mean? Is everything okay?" Tim explains that they're keeping her for observations, that she hasn't woken up yet from having another big seizure.

"They're going to do an ultrasound and check out the baby, try to figure out how far along she is. Her neurologist has to consult with some of the high-risk obstetricians to figure out a plan... basically they can't do anything until business hours tomorrow."

"Business hours? What is that—a bank? Fuck that shit! Tell them to get in the lab right now." I look over at Juniper, still sleeping in our bed. "Do you need me to come in there and be famous?"

Tim sighs. "Not tonight, brother. There isn't much they can do until Emma wakes up, anyway. But maybe you can come spell me sitting with Thatcher? Alice and I have to get home and get Petey...when do you leave for Denver?"

"Fuck." My flight leaves in a few hours. Now *I'm* kicking the couch. My family needs me, my wife needs me. Everything is falling apart.

Chapter 6

Thatcher

Nicole insists we wait for Emma to wake up before they do the ultrasound, even though the doc says they can roll a cart in here right now and check things out. Nicole gets right up in my face, flaring her nostrils at me, and I'm about to lose my damn mind when Tim and Alice rush into the room.

He puts a hand on my shoulder and I tense my whole body, not sure if I want to punch him just to release all this energy, or collapse against him like I'm ten years old and he's the only one I can lean on.

Tim pulls me into a hug and says, "We are going to figure all this out, Thatcher. All of us.

Together." Alice grabs my hand and rubs my thumb and my breathing slows a little bit. I'm not sure how much time passes. Tim and Alice and Nicole cycle in and out, taking turns sitting with me by Emma's bed, and I guess camping out in the waiting room. Who even knows.

It feels like one hundred years before Emma groans and opens her eyes, curling up in a ball on her side. "Shhh, Chezz." I put my face next to hers on the bed, my hand stroking her hair. I remember that she had terrible muscle aches the last time she had a seizure and I wonder if I should buzz someone to bring her any pain meds. "Emma, talk to me, please."

Her mouth works up and down, and side to side, before she meets my eyes and says, "Thatcher." A single tear spills out from one eye, and I bite my lip, wanting to take all this away from her and knowing I can't. "I thought I was done having seizures. I thought I was going to be normal." She starts to cry, and I kiss her forehead, trying to soothe her with gentle touches.

"You are perfect, Emma. You know that, right? You're perfect to me. You're my everything." I climb into the bed and try to scoop her into my lap without disrupting her IV, but all the commotion sets off a series of beeps on her IV pole. It's probably just as well, because the nurse comes in, so I ask her if there's anything she can give Emma for her aching muscles.

The nurse frowns at me, but I'm not going to leave my Chezz and climb out of this bed without a fight. "Can you go get Dr. Khalsa?" My voice is sharper than I intend, but I've never had a pregnant girlfriend before and fuck everyone standing in the way of me knowing answers.

Emma settles in against my shoulder and asks me what happened. I'm not sure if she remembers the fight we were having before her seizure, but I leave that part out and ensure her I called her doctor right away and drove her here to meet with him. "I actually don't know how long ago that was, Chezz. I think it might be morning by now..."

Nicole and, inexplicably, Ty come into the room just then. "Emma!" Ty crouches by the bed so she doesn't have to look up at his big, tall mug. "Listen. I have to fly out in like fifteen minutes, but I couldn't leave town without coming in to see if you were doing okay."

"Well, Ty," she says, grinning, "I feel like shit. But I appreciate you making a pit stop for little old me. Tell me what's going on out there." Emma gestures toward the waiting room while Nicole chugs coffee and taps her foot.

Ty smiles one of his devilish grins. "Did you see Juniper got a tattoo?" Emma nods. "It's fucking hot. You should get one, too." He winks at Emma. "When you're done being pregnant, obviously."

Fuck. I feel Emma stiffen. Her eyes widen and her voice seeps out in a whisper. "What?"

"Aw shit. Did I screw up?" Ty stands up, his joints popping, as Nicole swats him in the stomach.

"Get the fuck out of here and go win a hockey game, Tyrion," she says, capturing my sentiments. "Listen, Ems." Nicole sits on the bed and squeezes Emma's hand. "Dr. Khalsa thinks you had a seizure because your body is adjusting to rapidly shifting hormones."

"What are you talking about? Thatcher, what the hell do you guys know?"

Nicole raises her eyebrows. I sigh. "Emma, babe." I rub her shoulder and meet her eyes. Her pupils are tiny and I can tell she's terrified. "They did a bunch of tests when you came in, just to rule stuff out. One of them was a pregnancy test, sweetheart. And it was positive."

She starts shaking her head. "Nope. No. I'm on the pill." She looks at Nicole. "I always take my meds. I never miss my meds! I don't fucking drink. I set timers. I have little pill trays all sectioned out."

"Dr. Khalsa was saying that antibiotic you were on a little while ago might have made your birth control pills ineffective," I tell her. I'm not sure how I feel about how upset she seems, but then again, I'd be pissed too if people had conversations about me while I was passed out.

"Thatcher," she looks up at me. "That was two months ago." I nod. "So I'm two months pregnant? That's like...really pregnant..."

I weave my fingers through hers and raise her hand to kiss it gently. By this time, Ty has left but Tim and Alice have wandered back in along with Nicole, so the room is really fucking crowded when Dr. Khalsa pops his head in with a thin woman in scrubs. "Ah! Emma! I heard you were up," he says. "This is Dr. Elizabeth Hudson, one of our high-risk obstetricians."

Emma's eyes shoot around the room, flitting between all the doctors and Stags and Nicole. Dr. Hudson shakes Emma's hand and pulls a small machine out of her pocket. "Emma, if Dr. Khalsa's theory about your pregnancy is accurate, you should be far enough along that I could pick up a heartbeat on this device. If you could raise your gown we could check things out, make sure everything is okay with Baby."

Emma shakes her head, and I frown. I move to help her raise her gown but she swats my hand out of the way. "I'm not doing that," she says.

"Chezz," I start, sliding off the edge of the bed. "Come on. We have to see if the baby is okay after your seizure. I'm fucking dying here not knowing."

Emma meets my eye and I see a fury unlike she's shown me for a long time. She grits her teeth and says, through a locked jaw, "It doesn't matter if it's fine because I'm not going to stay pregnant."

Chapter 7

Ty

I played one hell of a game tonight. God, it feels good to sink a goal right through the five-hole, take the goalie off guard and watch that signal light up when the puck hits the net. My teammates pound me on the shoulder as we all walk back to the locker room afterward, and I wonder why the fuck I'm not feeling more excited.

We haven't lost a game yet, which I know isn't saying much because it's barely November, but I should be on a huge high after scoring and helping maintain our streak. Some members of the press stop me in the hall on my way to the locker room. The reporter seems comically short standing on the ground next to me in my skates, but it's their choice not to wait for me until I've showered.

"Ty, how's it feel to score your two hundred-fiftieth goal for the NHL?"

"Was tonight 250? I seriously hadn't been keeping track. I've just been loving playing for the Fury and as you know, I've got a great group of guys out there with me." It's weird that I didn't realize I was close to that milestone. This is my tenth year of pro hockey. I signed right out of high school. Shit, I'm getting old. The reporter is blinking at me and I realize I missed a question. "I'm sorry. I'm still letting it sink in that I shot 250 goals. Could you repeat the question?" I flash my two-dimple smile and I know they'll forgive anything.

"Sure thing, Ty. We asked what you think about the election. Your wife running for judge?"

"Aw man, my wife is going to be an amazing judge! She's a ferocious lawyer and loves defending the underdog in court. It just so happens we have an off day on Election Day, so I'll be thrilled to stand by her side while the numbers come in."

The reporter looks at me confused. "You're not worried her career will get in the way of your playoff hopes?"

Now it's my turn to be confused. "How so? You know we made it to the quarterfinals the year my wife took Olympic gold in rowing, right?" The reporter starts to make some comment, but I cut them off. "Listen. Juniper Jones is a force of nature. I'm so fucking proud of her. We push each other. Now, if you'll excuse me, I've gotta go shower."

I hate these interviews. What do they want me to say? That I'd rather have some puck bunny who lives for my career and follows me everywhere? Honestly, I've had my share of those women. Juniper is my soul mate. I don't give a shit if that sounds cheesy. I felt a connection with her that first minute we met. I don't need her doting on me. I just need her to be herself.

I hurry through the showers and find a quiet room to call home. Shit's been insane with my family and I haven't been in Pittsburgh at all to help with any of it. My brother Tim is losing his mind at Juniper leaving the firm and Thatcher is freaking the fuck out because Emma says she doesn't want to keep the baby. Something about pregnancy being too high risk with her epilepsy.

I don't know what to say to any of them. All I know is when I call Juniper, she can tell me about her campaign stuff and I can pretend I understand what she's talking about, and remind her that she's got my vote. Always.

I look at the time as the phone rings and rings. Juniper isn't picking up. It's not that late. We put away that game in under three hours. "Hello?" she finally answers, and I can tell I woke her up.

"Aw, JJ, I'm sorry. Were you asleep?"

"Shit," she says. "I don't know why I'm this tired. I mean, I've been going hard but not *that* hard. I didn't even row today."

"You missed your workout?" Juniper has never missed a workout since I've known her. She holds meetings from the indoor rowing machine sometimes if shit is really busy, with her assistant taking notes while Juniper bangs out a few miles. "You feeling okay, babe?"

"Hmm," she says. "I guess I'm not. I'm really run down. When are you back?"

I promise her I'll take the red-eye, fly home before the team. My JJ needs me. "I'm going to take you to the doctor tomorrow morning. Get some sleep, babe. Whatever you were going to do tonight can wait." She yawns, and I try not to worry. I clean out my hotel room quickly and text my manager that I'm skipping town early. As I hail a cab to the airport, I feel this sinking sense of dread that I'm not where I'm supposed to be.

I know this is my job. It's not like I'm out of town getting laid or sitting on the beach somewhere. But my family needs me and I'm not there. That's not okay. They've all come to expect me to not be helpful, and more and more, that pisses me off. I stare out the window, thinking how much my shoulder hurts and how empty my win feels knowing the people I love are hurting, and there's not a damn thing I can do about it.

Juniper is out cold when I get home, and in the furor of Election Day, she won't agree to go with me to the doctor in the morning. We walk to the polls together and I don't even pull on a baseball cap. I want to be seen voting for my JJ. I hear some of the poll workers explaining to people in line that they can't just show up here to vote— they have to go vote in their own neighborhood. Once I click the button I walk over and sign some autographs, encourage them to go back to make their vote count.

Some of them follow us when we start driving to her campaign headquarters, but I don't mind that either. I promise Juniper I'll put them all to work for her when we arrive. It weighs on me that she has dark circles under her eyes. Alice is chipper as always, greeting us with breakfast sandwiches and batches of hot coffee, but I see her frown when Juniper runs off to the bathroom to throw up. "It's just nerves, right?" I ask my brother Tim. He scratches his chin and makes eye contact with Alice. Whatever. I don't have time to interpret their secret eyeball language.

I start making calls for Juniper. I love this part of helping her campaign. Every time I get a potential voter on the phone, I reassure them that yes, it's really me. Yes, hockey players care about political stuff...it helps when my hot-ass wife is the one running for office.

By midday, it seems like we are doing really well and I convince Juniper to come sit and have a sandwich. She really seems to perk up after that.

I spend some time goofing off with my brothers around the campaign office. I can't think of the last time we all spent time together like this. It must have been since before preseason started for me.

Emma stayed home today. Thatcher said she doesn't want to get involved, since her dad is running for reelection, too, and she kind of hates her dad. We don't talk about the pregnancy thing. From what Tim said, Emma still doesn't want to go through with it...but she's sort of on a timeline for when she has to make that choice. My guts ache for Thatcher, thinking about his position right now. It's not like he's always wanted to be a dad, but he and Emma have a good thing going. He's really great with our nephew. I shake my head and get back to the phones. No time to worry about all this stuff today.

* * *

The polls close at eight and Juniper is nowhere to be seen. Some folks are here from the news, which makes me really wish we had Emma around, because she knows how to talk to these reporters. Emma works for a huge newspaper and her writing is the main reason I ever read anything anymore. Television reporters give Emma more space if she's ever hanging around me, since she works with them at the *Post*.

I guess I'm the next best thing to Juniper, wherever she is, and I sidle up to talk to the press. "Hey, guys, what's the good news?" I ask them, hoping I can buy some time until my wife turns up. *Where the hell would she go right now? I wonder.*

I shoot the shit with some of the reporters, trying to keep the conversation related to the Fury since I have no idea how to talk about politics stuff. It's a little weird to me that being a judge is something you have to get voted into, not promoted. But whatever, Juniper will kick ass either way. I'm neck-deep in a conversation about our playoff potential for this season when I finally see Juniper coming down the hallway. She must have been in the back doing...god knows what.

Her campaign manager-slash-rowing coach runs up and grabs her arm. He shouts excitedly, "Did you see the reports, Juniper? You're in!"

She doesn't answer him. She must be overcome with happiness. I can relate. Sometimes it takes a minute for good news to sink in. She makes a face at me, connects with my eyes and locks me in place with her stare. "JJ," I say, walking toward her. "Did you hear Derek? You won, babe."

"I'm pregnant," she says, and I look down to see she's holding a white plastic stick. Camera flashes start popping and all the sound leaves as the walls close in around me. The stick in her hand says *pregnant* in bright blue letters.

Chapter 8
Tim

Alice shakes me awake much earlier than I need to be up. We are supposed to go buy a Christmas tree later, even though it's not December yet. Alice insists we need the tree up and decorated by the time we host Thanksgiving here and I'm trying not to think about all those people in my house *plus* having to string lights and sweep up tree needles.

"Babe, it's not even light out yet," I grumble, but she plunks Petey on my stomach and there's no going back to sleep after that. He starts patting my face and pulling my hair, so I pretend I'm a grizzly bear and growl at him for awhile until I hear the magic words from downstairs.

"Guys! Breakfast is ready!"

"What do you say, Champ?" I ask Petey, tossing him upside down over my shoulder.

"Let's eeeeeeeeeat!" he yells as I jiggle him around. We pass my grandmother in the hall on our way past and she smiles. I love seeing the look in her eyes when she sees me with my son. I just never imagined this part of my future, and so each day that I'm here with my family in a home—a real home, not just a house—it feels like a dream I never even hoped to wish for. I kiss my Gram on the cheek.

"Timber," she says, pulling up a chair in the dining room. "I think you need to go talk to Emma."

I raise an eyebrow at her. "Pretty sure Thatcher has that under control, Gram. Alice, this is amazing." She made muffins and sliced strawberries, although Petey has eaten most of those by the time I reach over to grab the bowl.

My grandmother shakes her head. "Thatcher's panicking. Emma is, too. You're good in a crisis." Grabbing a plate and a coffee, she heads back upstairs without a look back. That's her MO. She drops truth bombs and takes off to play bridge online.

Alice sits next to me and rubs my leg while I chew. "I think she might be right," she says.

Talking with my mouth full, I ask, "Shouldn't *you* talk to her? You're the one who experienced getting pregnant unexpectedly!"

Alice nods and ponders that for a minute. "Yeah," she says. "That's true, Tim, but I think your grandma is right about this. Emma listens to you, in a competitive, wise-old-man type of way."

I sigh. "Obviously I'm biased here. She's pregnant with a Stag child and they're financially secure and, you remember, Alice, I have connections with some high-risk obstetricians. I've been doing some research..."

"Of course you have, Tim," she says. "That's why I love you. I also think you've been researching this to avoid thinking about having to replace Juniper at work. And that's okay, too. You don't need to solve all your problems at once." I snort, and Alice stands up to start working on tying her curls back in a ponytail. It takes her awhile, and I love staring at her while she does it. She laughs and kisses my cheek. "Go talk to Emma, and ask Thatcher to borrow his truck so you can get the tree." Scooping up our son, she nuzzles his nose and climbs upstairs to wrestle him into some clothes. "I'll make you some caramel sauce while you're gone."

She winks at me and disappears. I guess she's right that I should go see my brother.

I grab a muffin and stick it in a paper bag, then grab a second one for Thatcher so it doesn't look like I'm a total asshole barging in on them before eight in the morning.

* * *

By the time I get to their house, though, I see that I'm not their first visitor. Thatcher had bought a double lot on the north side of the city to renovate into a glass studio and living space. He put in a carport on the side lot with a little fenced-in patio. I can't help but think how nice that would be for a little Stag kid to run around outside, maybe hang out with Petey. We don't bring him over here much, but I should probably change that. "Maybe Thatcher and Emma should host Thanksgiving," I mutter, blowing a cold breath into my fist. I wish I'd worn some gloves.

I park next to an unfamiliar black coupe and punch in the code to get inside. As I climb up to the loft, I hear a familiar voice. Emma's friend Nicole is yelling, "It all sounds like bullshit to me, Ems." Before I can decide whether to knock or eavesdrop, the door to the loft slides open and Nicole whips her head in my direction. "Oh, Christ, it's you," she sighs. "I guess you're here to talk sense into her, too."

I'm not sure what to say here, especially since I don't know what Nicole is talking about specifically, so I hold out the bag. "Alice sent muffins!" My voice is falsely cheerful as I try to assess this situation as I might a difficult courtroom.

Nicole snatches the bag from my hand and peers inside. She takes a muffin and tosses the bag to Emma, who is sprawled on the couch looking green. "Eat this," Nicole says. "I think you can keep it down." Changing her direction back to me, Nicole takes a bite, and says, "I take it you're *really* here to talk to Emma, though." I nod. "Good," she says. "We've got a small window here to make a decision and I don't believe Emma is approaching said decision properly."

"What do you mean?" Emma groans and runs into the bathroom. Nicole grins and walks over to the counter, where I see she has set out a giant pad of paper.

"Decisions require strategy," she says. "In any situation, you must lay out all the elements, weigh pros and cons, and take insight from all stakeholders." I see that Nicole has begun to write a lot of this down. I pull up a stool and nod for her to continue. "Now," she says, "Nobody is going to tell Emma what to do here. But I'd like to make sure she has approached this systematically." I see phrases like "health risk—comparatively minor" and "co-parenting potential—extraordinarily high."

Emma staggers back from the bathroom and Nicole hands her some water. "Are you ready to hear the rest of my presentation?" Emma rolls her eyes and nods. I sit back with my arms crossed as Nicole pulls out sheets of research study summaries. She tells Emma all about the risks of pregnancy for women with epilepsy, and counters each risk with information about resources available here in Pittsburgh. My jaw drops. I've never seen anyone so prepared for an argument since...well, since I put myself through law school. This is a master class on debate.

"Moving on," Nicole says, flipping the page. She's printed an unflattering picture of Thatcher and taped it to the paper. "Thatcher Stag has already won me over as a partner for you." She looks at Emma. "We've been over this part before, but now we have an audience, so I'm reviewing." Emma groans again while Nicole points out that Thatcher has a tendency toward crabbiness, but finds thoughtful gifts, is great with his nephew, and "the man doles out hundreds of orgasms, Ems." Nicole taps a pencil on the counter as Emma turns scarlet. I cough, uncomfortably. I suppose it's good to know my brother is a thoughtful lover. *Where the hell are these thoughts coming from,* I think, looking around for something else to focus on in my brother's apartment, with his pregnant fiancée looking nauseous.

"The way I see it," Nicole continues, "On paper, this pregnancy gets the green light. So I'm waiting for a rational rebuttal from you, Emma, because I've been over and over all of this and my advice to you would be to proceed."

Emma looks at me, and there's something in her eyes I can't place. "I'm scared," she whispers. "I'm scared of so many things. Like, what if I have a major seizure and cause brain damage to the baby? And what if..." she drifts off. "What if I'm a shitty mom?" As she says this, she begins to cry and I remember what Thatcher told me about her own mother's coldness, and her preference for Emma's older sister.

I came over here expecting to use logic and try to argue with Emma, but I see now that she just really needs a hug. I slip into another role I've been playing for decades, since my mother died. I wrap my arms around her and whisper into her hair. "I'm here. I will help you. Everything will be fine, Emma." She cries into my chest as I think about Alice, so confident in her mothering because she had such a vibrant mother and the close support of her huge family. "We are all here with you, Emma. All of us." I lift her chin and meet her eyes with my own. "You're a Stag now."

Chapter 9

Thatcher

I open the door to my house to see Nicole staring at my brother, who is cradling Emma. "What the hell is everyone crying about," I say. As it's falling out of my mouth, I know I'm just proving everyone right who thinks I'm a cranky old bastard. This whole thing is fucking with my head. Emma won't even talk to me half the time, and it's killing me.

She's pregnant, carrying a tiny Stag baby. My fucking baby. And she won't talk about it since her stay in the hospital when she said she wasn't sure if she'd keep the pregnancy. I keep thinking back to our argument before she had the seizure. I know she's right—I haven't been doing a good job showing her how I feel about her. How she's my everything. The only person half the time who keeps me from being a hermit with no friends.

There's no use dancing into this, so I just blurt, "Emma, you're the light of my life," and everyone whips their head around to stare at me. I ignore all of them but Emma. "Can I show you something?"

Nobody says anything, but Tim lets go of my girl and wipes at his eye. "Hey, man," he says, patting me on the shoulder. Apparently Emma is going to make me work to get her to come see my surprise. I shake off my coat and hang it on a hook as he keeps talking. Something about Christmas trees and Alice and Thanksgiving dinner. "So can I borrow your truck?"

"What?"

"Your truck. The old beater...white stick-shift piece-of-shit truck? Can I borrow it?"

I have to laugh at the thought of Tim driving my truck when he's told me a thousand times that it's not up to his safety standards. "No can do, Timmy. Sorry."

"You don't have to be a dick, Thatcher. Alice asked me not to get pine needles in the Volvo."

Emma sniffs and I look over at her, meeting her gaze. "I can't lend you the truck because I got rid of it this morning," I say. I hold out a set of keys for Emma to see. "I wanted to get something safer. Something better for a family."

Nobody talks for a minute and I feel the crisp breeze come through the sliding door to our loft. "You sold the truck?" Emma's voice is a whisper. "You love that truck."

I nod and close the distance between us. God, it always feels so good to hold her. Her scent washes over me as I suck in great lungfuls of Emma. "I love you more," I say. I can practically hear Tim rolling his eyes at me. Emma lets me hug her and I pull her in, nestling my chin in her red hair, rubbing her back. She smells a little bit like peppermint today, and I'm glad she's been drinking the tea I got her to settle her stomach.

In the background, I hear Nicole clicking her tongue at my brother. "What's the point of being filthy rich if you're not going to take advantage of the service industry," she scolds. I hear her clicking around on her phone. "Look," she says, shoving her phone in Tim's face as I pet Emma's hair. "This tree place delivers."

"How about the two of you get out of here and let me talk to Emma in peace," I say, squeezing her shoulders. "I want to show her my new family wagon. Which I had to park on the street, by the way, because there's no room in my own damn carport."

Tim and Nicole make their way out as Emma starts to cry softly against my shoulder. "Talk to me, Chezz," I tell her. "I'm dying without you."

"I'm scared, Thatcher." Her voice is muffled in my shirt.

"I know you are. I'm scared, too. God, I'm so scared something will happen to you. Can we talk about it?"

I tip her face up so she meets my eye. Her cheeks are wet with tears and I hate that. I don't think she's cried since we were first together, when we were just pretending to be a couple, and I was too dumb to communicate my feelings to her. "I will do anything for you, Emma," I assure her. "Can we read the stuff your doctors sent?"

She lets me guide her over to the couch and we read over some of the pamphlets from the OB. My mind keeps wandering between our argument and the idea of her growing my baby inside her. Finally, I can't take it anymore. "Emma," I say. "I want to show you our new car."

She raises an eyebrow at me. I sigh. "I wanted to do something...a gesture. I want to show you I'm all-in here. I want to be your in-case-of-emergency person at the hospital, and I want you to know I'm a serious adult capable of being a dad. And I want you to know that you're it for me."

I grab her coat and start wrapping it around her so I can walk her downstairs. "Take a ride with me, Emma." She looks at the silver Audi SUV I bought and snorts.

"That's quite an upgrade, Stag," she says. "Did they laugh at you when you traded in the truck?" She punches my arm playfully and I open the door for her to climb in.

"I'll have you know I sold the truck to Cody at a discounted rate," I tell her. "I can't very well haul glass supplies around in my new family vehicle."

Emma sits in the leather interior, looking around at all the fancy-ass features I don't even know if we need. I just told the guy at the dealership I wanted the best car for a family. As per usual, he took one look at my ink and my ripped jeans and thought I was taking him for a ride, but I pulled out my Black Amex card and all of a sudden he was sweet as pie. I did all right for myself before I started doing work for the hottest new architect in Pittsburgh, but my commission last year really set Stag Glass up in the big leagues. I have more money than sense, Tim keeps telling me. Now I'm going to spend some of it on Emma.

"Hey, Em," I tell her, tucking some of her wild red hair behind her ear. "Even if...I want you to know I think you should be riding around in this kind of car." I swallow. I can't even bring myself to talk about what she said at the hospital. I can't say those words out loud. "There are so many air bags in here, babe. I should have upgraded for you a long time ago. Kept the truck just for deliveries." She smiles. "Should we go show your parents?"

That brings out a laugh. She hasn't even told them anything yet. I know we're supposed to see them for brunch soon, since we will be with my family for Thanksgiving dinner. Emma has been avoiding talking about it, and I know she doesn't want to drive over there right now. She looks off into the distance and shivers a little. I start the engine and turn on her seat heater for her. "Can we go spy on Tim and Alice picking out a Christmas tree?" she asks.

I grin and put the car in gear. "Abso-fucking-lutely."

Chapter 10

Ty

Juniper and I have been staring at each other across our kitchen table for a few days. Every now and then, one of us will say, "Pregnant. Hmm." It's such a fucking weird feeling. We made a human. Not even on purpose. It seemed hilarious when this happened to Tim. Now that it's me about to be a dad? Everything is swirling around in my head. Like Christmas. It's almost Christmas. Next year at this time I'll be buying presents for a kid and playing Santa and all that. And who even knows if I'll be in town for the kid's first Christmas. I'm on the road all the fucking time for hockey. It's not like Juniper can pack up and come with me. She has a fucking career. And you can't just have a baby go through time zones and stuff.

"Judge Juney," I say, slurping at my coffee.

"Hmm?"

"Judge Juney. I want to call you that, JJ." I smile at her. I'm so damn proud of my wife. She's a rock star. But we are barely holding our shit together over here. Both of us have really demanding jobs. I only just figured out about sending out laundry. How will a baby Stag fit into this madness? I scoot my chair closer to her and drop a hand on her thigh like nothing's happened. I just want to touch her, reassure myself that's she still there. Still real.

"What do we think about asking Becky for more help around here," I ask, waving my hand around our townhouse, where the dishes are piling high. Our housekeeper had been coming once a week for just a few hours, but if Juniper's going to be falling asleep at six p.m. and puking all morning, we are going to need more help. Especially if I'm on the road. I tug on my hair. It should be me here every morning by my wife's side, rubbing her back while she barfs. I guess until we figure out an answer, we can just get more help.

Juniper nods and says, "that's a really good idea, Ty." She sighs. "I have to go to the store. I need more crackers and stuff."

"I'll order that for you online," I tell her, tucking a piece of hair behind her ear. "We can have them delivered. You've got me all to yourself for like 18 more hours. Can we talk about...all of this?"

She sighs in deep, slow agreement and tells me, "I just keep thinking about my mom. I have no idea who she is. Or was?" Juniper grew up in a group home until her dad adopted her as a kid. We never did find out who her birth parents were. "I don't have any way to know if she got sick every day like this. If she had an easy birth... I have no history, Ty. How can I do this without history?"

"It's not a legal case, JJ. You don't need to find the precedent. We will figure it all out together." I lean in and kiss her forehead, then tug her onto my lap and rub her back while I can. "We will just ask Alice everything."

Resting my chin on the top of her head, I wonder about my own mom. Tim showed us the picture of her on the wall at the midwife place where Alice had Petey. Tim and Thatcher can remember mom pregnant with me, and I sure am jealous of that. But fuck. I can't wait to see what Juniper looks like pregnant with a little Staglet. "This baby is going to be so damn tall," I tell her, dropping a hand to her stomach. Her abs are still tight and firm. We did some math after the election and she's *just* a month pregnant. It must have happened on that stretch of home games where I was waking her up to celebrate every night in between her campaign stops and my preseason games. I smile, wondering if we made a baby on the kitchen floor or on the couch or in our bed.

"I can feel you thinking dirty thoughts, Tyrion Stag," she says, but she wraps her arms around me. I feel like the ice has been broken. Like we can be ourselves around each other again. "I guess I need to make a baby plan. Like when am I supposed to see a doctor?"

"Do you think you want to try seeing the midwives where my mom went?" I try not to sound desperate, but god damn, I want some connection with my family for all of this. I want to see that midwife who saw my mom through having all of us. "I'd like to at least go check them out. If that's okay," I tell her.

Juniper sighs again and tells me Alice has been pestering her to do that, too. "Alice says the baby will glide right out of me because I have powerful thighs," she laughs. But I figure that's probably true. Juniper is tough as hell. *At least the baby won't come until after the playoffs,* I think, looking at the wall calendar. I know for damn sure I wouldn't miss my kid being born, but it's definitely a lot easier knowing I don't have to dance around the pro hockey schedule.

Juniper pulls out her phone so we can look at the calendar and make some appointments. It feels better just having dates on the books. I'm going to have to miss some practice sessions, she's going to have to cut short her time at Stag Law, but we are going to figure this shit out. Together. By the time we finish, Juniper even feels up to a run, so we layer up and step outside into the crisp November air.

We aim small, since she's been feeling so lousy, deciding to stop for peppermint lattes at the coffee shop two miles from our house. It's just starting to get dark, and even though it's mid-November, a lot of people have put their lights up already. We fall in step beside one another, puffing out frosted breaths and spying on these picturesque houses already so immersed in the family feel of the holidays. It's easy to believe everything will be okay, sipping a warm, minty drink and holding hands beneath those glowing lights. We will figure it all out. Eventually.

Chapter 11
Tim

"You could at least help me with the ladder," I yell at Thatcher, who seems content enough to sit on the porch and watch me wrestling with the icicle lights Alice and Petey insisted we get. He laughs at me and tugs at his wool coat, blowing into his hand and walking over to steady the ladder. "I saw you and Emma spying on us," I tell him. They pulled up all smug in his new SUV to watch us tussle with the Christmas tree. Alice vetoed Nicole's idea of just ordering one for delivery. She wanted to go out there and chop one down like country tourists or something.

"You looked so manly with that saw, big bro," Thatcher says, laughing again. He's not wrong, though. It did feel good to whack through that tree, knock it over, and drag it up to the checkout area. I grunt in response as Thatcher helps unwind the strings of lights. "What's up with your Juniper situation?" he asks.

She hasn't really been working to her potential since Election Day, when she blurted out she was pregnant in front of the news cameras. It's all everyone talks about—how she will be Pittsburgh's first elected judge to take maternity leave this next spring, and would she still take the post.

"It's a circus," I tell him. "She's going to be fine. Stag Law, on the other hand..." I drift off. Juniper is not only a fine lawyer, but had been helping me shape the direction of the company. I've let myself become someone totally new in the past few years. I never used to give a fuck what other people thought or take a minute to assess their opinions. I never had the luxury of time to ponder. I was always too busy raising my brothers, making sure they made good grades and stayed out of trouble. When it came time to open my law business, I handled it the same way. Do. Achieve. I never bothered to rely on anyone else, and so I never felt fucked when someone left Stag Law to work elsewhere.

Meeting Alice...she took my breath away and taught me how to rely on other people. Share in the hard stuff *and* the good stuff. So what does it get me? I bring Juniper into the fold, grow a damn fine business at her side...and she leaves me. *Well.* I pause and tack some lights up on the eaves. She's not *leaving* me. She just reached the top of her potential with Stag Law. "Fuck it."

I climb down the ladder and toss the rope of lights to Thatcher. "Your turn, dick wad," I tell him. And before he can protest, I say, "this is for spying on me at the tree farm. Thatcher snorts and climbs up the ladder. Fuck him for hanging the lights faster than me. He works with his hands all day long. He's used to this shit.

"Hey," he calls down, talking around the nails in his teeth. "Is our father coming for Thanksgiving?"

"I guess so. I haven't talked to him in awhile." Things have been precarious with our father the past year or so. After he walked out on us and hid inside a bourbon bottle for 13 years, his body basically shut down. Thatcher found him in the hospital the last time Emma was in there with a seizure. "Gram talks him sort of regularly, I think. So I'm assuming he will be here." Ted Stag had finally gotten sober and has slowly been more involved in our lives. "What makes you ask about that?" My brother climbs down the ladder and we move it over a few feet to finish up the last of the lights.

"I want to ask him about when Mom was pregnant," Thatcher says with a shrug.

I don't ask him to elaborate or whether Emma has talked more about her pregnancy. "Sounds like a great topic for a big holiday gathering," I snort. If I'm honest, I'm the one who has warmed up to Ted the least since we reunited. Seems fair to me, since I'm the one who picked up all his work when he couldn't handle his grief at losing our mother. He's apologized and made amends, but it's a slow process. I'm working on it. I want him to know Alice and Petey. I just don't think to ask him for insight when I'm having a hard time in life.

I need to think about something else. Ted Stag reminds me how hard it is to rely on someone else and how big the disappointment feels when they inevitably let you down. I try to think about Alice. "Oh, hey. Alice was asking if Emma is having any aversions."

"What the fuck does that mean? Like how she doesn't drink alcohol?"

"Aversions. Like...things pregnant ladies can't handle. Alice couldn't walk past fast-food places when she was pregnant with Petey. The smell of the fried oil made her sick to her stomach."

"Hmm." Thatcher nails in the final end of the lights and reaches out for the extension cord. I pass it up to him as he says, "She won't talk about it yet. I don't want to push her."

I plug in the cord and step back. In the late afternoon, we can just see the glow of the lights around the overhang from the front porch. Alice has stuck bunches of greens out the windows on the second and third floor, putting candles in the windows. The house looks like a fairy-tale house. "Mom used to do that," I say. "Put greens in the windows."

Thatcher nods. "I remember. She'd like these icicle things." He throws an arm around my shoulder, and I let him. The scent of pine drifts down in the crisp air. It's nice. It feels right. We stand there admiring the scene until I hear the door fling open. Petey and my nephews spill out of the house, running and screaming, while Alice and Amy climb down the porch steps to admire our work.

"It looks magical, babe," Alice says, kissing my cheek. I hadn't realized how cold I've gotten until her warm lips press against my skin. Something about the mood makes me pull her in close, longing to cocoon into the couch and just hold her while I figure out the answer to everything. I need her to remind me, again, that it's okay to trust other people. That the risk can be worthwhile.

The boys start throwing sticks at each other and Thatcher gets down low, playing with them, pretending he's an abominable snowman. I look up and see my grandmother smiling down from her room on the third floor. For now, everything here is as it should be. All of us together. Happy. Loud. Then I remember Thatcher's question about our father and head inside to check with Gram.

She pats my hand and tells me Ted will indeed be joining us. So we will have two Stag women with unplanned pregnancies, me trying to figure out the future of my business, Alice running around like mad, cooking insane foods...this will be a Stag family Thanksgiving to remember.

Chapter 12

Thatcher

Emma bursts into my studio, startling me so that I almost drop the rod with molten glass on the end. "Chezz," I scold her, clucking my tongue. "That was almost a very painful greeting." I roll the rod back and forth with one hand, shaping the glass a bit and trying to urge it into the look I'd imagined. "What's up, babe?"

She bites her lip and sits on a stool, but she's fidgeting so badly I can tell she's going to explode if I don't talk to her soon. "Come over here," I say, holding out an arm. She stands in front of me and I hand her the rod, propped up on one end of my workbench. "Hold this." She smiles at me and rolls the blob of glass back and forth as I squat on the ground next to her. I hold her gaze while I blow gently into the hollow tube, creating just enough space in the glass to achieve a teardrop shape. She makes a lewd face at me and I laugh. Glass blowing has no shortage of innuendo. I love having Emma in my studio with me when I'm thinking about hot rods and blowing tubes. Then I remember that there isn't much blowing or bumping between us lately. *Damn.*

I put my hand over hers and tap the drop off the end and, settling one hand on her back, grab the glass with metal tongs. I carry it into the kiln to cool down, close the door, and pull her against me. She lets me, and I feel relieved. Like maybe we are chipping away a few inches of whatever wall got built up near the tattoo shop that day. "Tell me what's got you so excited," I whisper into the shell of her ear, planting a kiss on her neck, just below her lobe. She shivers slightly and leans back to look at me.

"I won a Press Award," she breathes. Then she can't contain herself anymore and starts jumping and clapping her hands. "I just met with Phil and he told me."

She doesn't need to explain to me that this is a big-fucking-deal writing award. Those honors come with thousands of dollars in prize money and a trip to a swanky ceremony in New York City. I try to imagine Emma's gruff editor telling her the biggest news that might ever come to the *Pittsburgh Post*.

"For your prison story?" I ask, remembering all the nights I drove her to and from the county jail to meet with guards and inmates and talk about pregnancy behind bars. Emma nods, twirling around, still jumping. She's about to publish the last installment of her series and has basically been working around the clock for months. Until recently, of course.

"Thatcher." She stops. "Phil wants me to expand it into a book."

"That's amazing, Emma." I pull her hand to my lips, kissing her palm gently. I'm so proud of my girl. I imagine how hot she'd look on a book jacket cover, her red hair pulled back in a smooth braid. Emma is so smart, always notices the most interesting details and writes them into her stories. "Can we celebrate?"

She nods, tugging my hand. "But let me tell you!" Gesturing wildly, Emma starts describing how the prize isn't just about prestige. Her editor thinks she should take a sabbatical from reporting. Devote a whole year into expanding her work into a book. He even apparently smiled at her and used positive adjectives during their meeting.

I grin. "It's kind of spooky timing, isn't it," I ask her. "You write about pregnancy in awful circumstances, while you're pregnant..."

The light fades from her eyes almost immediately. "I haven't even told my editor about...anything. Yet."

I swallow and take her hands. "Emma," I say. "Talk to me. What are you feeling right now? Because, Chezz, you have so much support. You have so many people rooting for you, wanting to help you stay healthy through all this. I will do *anything* you need."

She bites the side of her lip and looks into the flame in my furnace. "I never thought about how me being pregnant related to a research project about pregnant inmates. Writing a book could be good," she pauses. "If I'm having health problems. I mean it'd be a little more flexible than having to meet deadlines and stuff."

I rub her hand, not bothering to pull away just because I notice my hands are dirty from my work. "Dr. Khalsa said he feels confident he could keep you feeling pretty healthy," I say, remembering our conversation in his office. I went in to see him with Emma this past week after Juniper's news broke. Dr. Khalsa pulled up studies on pregnancy and epilepsy. Many of the women in his case studies had less control of their symptoms than Emma.

"I hate having seizures, Thatcher," she says. Her eyes swell with tears as she looks at me.

"I know you do, Chezz. I wish I could take that away from you." And I've never meant anything more earnestly. I'd take on her suffering in a heartbeat, just to give her a day not to worry about that feeling washing over her. "I know you hate losing control like that." She nods. I pull her onto my lap on the stool and cradle her into my arms. "How do you feel today?"

We talk a little longer about her nausea. I brave the question from Alice, about anything to avoid at Thanksgiving. When Emma tells me the smell of tomatoes has been making her sick, it feels like a nugget of treasure. A piece of information about her pregnancy that I want to cherish, because I've felt so in the dark these past few weeks. We talk until I hear her stomach growl, and I close up shop.

We slide into the sleek interior of my new car and drive to get sandwiches, and I try not to think too much about what it would be like to have a tiny baby Stag in the back seat for a fast-food run. When Emma turns on the Christmas radio station, I don't even roll my eyes. It just feels right to drive around with her humming "Carol of the Bells" until we roll up to the sandwich shop. The guy at the drive-through window even talks me into a tray of gingerbread for dessert. Something about the traditions of the season make our worries fade a bit. Emma's eyes gleam at the sound of the gingerbread, so I order a double and laugh as she dives into her portion while we're driving home.

We settle in to eat at the kitchen table, and it feels so familiar, so right. We haven't had this lightness and ease in our interactions in a few weeks. She looks longingly over at my sandwich —her favorite and mine. I introduced her to this sub shop when we started getting together. But Emma isn't supposed to have deli meat while she's pregnant—she's been reading all the stuff the doctors sent home with her—and she frowns at my ham sandwich while she picks at her grilled chicken. It feels so good to tease her, and I make moaning sounds while she feigns anger. I let her have my portion of dessert.

"So," I say after we eat, trying not to talk her way so she doesn't have to smell my ham breath. "What do you want to do to celebrate your award? Maybe a nice meal at the country club?"

Emma smacks me in the arm and rolls her eyes. I lean back in my chair, nursing a beer while Emma clutches her teacup. She blushes. "I can think of something I'd like," she says.

I raise an eyebrow, wanting to be right about what that facial expression from her usually means. "You're going to have to be really direct, Chezz. It's been a hell of a few weeks."

She doesn't say anything, but stands up and walks slowly toward me, her fingers trailing along the table. "I want you, Thatcher," she says, licking her bottom lip and meeting my eye. She nestles herself in between my legs in front of the chair and my dick springs to life in my pants. The soft light in our kitchen brings out the golden tones in her hair and she looks like a glimmering goddess. I set my beer bottle on the table and put my hands on her hips, my thumbs gently stroking her thighs through her jeans.

"I want you, too, Emma. So fucking bad. Are you sure, baby?"

She nods and reaches for the hem of her shirt. She lifts it slowly over her head, giving me the first glimpse of the subtle ways her body has changed in just the past few weeks. Three months pregnant, Emma seems...fuller somehow. Her flat stomach strains a bit, with the hint of a swell right at the waistband of her jeans. Her chest rises and falls slowly as she breathes, and I keep my hands on her hips, afraid to touch her. I look at her breasts, mesmerized. They have grown noticeably and spill over the cups of her bra. She takes my breath away, but I swallow and manage to say, "Emma. You're gorgeous."

She grips my face in her hands and leans in, kissing me deeply, and I moan softly against her full lips. Christ, I've missed this. I let my tongue slip into her mouth, exploring the corners like they're mine to dominate. I break the kiss. "I should never take you for granted, Chezz."

She's breathing heavy and her lips look swollen from the force of our kiss. She grabs my hands from her hips and places them on her chest. "Thatcher," she says, a spark in her eye. "Shut up and just fuck me already."

I stand up quickly, tipping the chair behind me. At my full height I tower over her, and I stoop to pick her up. I need space to ravish her properly, so I lift her up against me, grinding her center against my hard length. She wraps her arms around my neck and hooks her ankles behind my back as I carry her down the hall toward our room.

Stumbling in the dark, I don't want to take time to turn on the lights. I grow desperate, the past few weeks of our emotional distance surging inside me until my body throbs with need. Stumbling onto the bed, I laugh as she falls beneath me. Emma twists away just enough to peel off the rest of her clothes and I hurry to join her. As I unhook my belt and unzip my jeans, I gasp. Emma thrusts out a hand and wraps it around my cock. I hiss at the feel of her cool skin against my shaft. I fit so perfectly in her hand. Bracing my weight on my forearms, I lean over her, and Emma guides my tip toward her core.

"I'm so wet, Thatcher," she says. "Whenever I'm not puking, I'm horny as fuck."

To illustrate her point, she rubs the tip of my dick against her seam and I feel just how wet she is. "You're soaked, Chezz," I say. "And I've been hard every fucking day looking at you." I start to slide inside, slowly, giving her time to adjust to me. I meet her eye and, just like every day, I know I'm supposed to be here. Right here. I slide deeper now, until Emma grabs my hips and pulls me tight against her. I feel her nipples on my chest, taut and so hard.

She rocks her body against me and I almost lose my mind, she feels so damn good. But it's not just that it feels good physically. Emma is my muse. She grounds me, calls me out on my bullshit when I'm being a cranky asshole. She works twice as hard as anybody else every single day, simply because she's keeping her shit together so she doesn't have a seizure.

"Emma…" I'm panting now. "I love you so much, babe. I need you. Always."

She's moaning now, grinding against me so my body stimulates her right where she needs it. Emma starts groaning when I dip my hips, letting my groin rub against her needy clit. "I have to see you come, Chezz," I whisper, leaning toward her ear. I bite it gently, letting my teeth sink into her lobe while I press into her harder.

"Fuck! Thatcher! God, yes!" Emma locks her eyes on to mine and I can see the moment she falls over the edge, even as I feel her pulsing, her muscles contracting all around me. Before I know what's happening, I lose myself. The pleasure washes through me and I explode inside her while she twitches in the aftershocks of her orgasm.

"Gah!" I bellow out with a final gasp, thrusting once more before collapsing on top of Emma. And then I immediately get scared I'm going to hurt her and the baby, and I roll us over so she's on her side on top of me.

"What's with the gymnastics?" Emma brushes her wild red hair out of her face, sticky with sweat.

I shrug, afraid to spoil the moment and bring up the pregnancy. She still hasn't *said* that she's going to go through with everything, even though I think the window has passed when she had to make that choice. I fall asleep with her in my arms, determined to keep her there, wondering what I need to do to help her feel safe.

Chapter 13

Tim

I never thought I'd enjoy Thanksgiving dinner. For so many years, it was just my brothers and my grandmother and me trying to figure out some stovetop stuffing and a frozen turkey breast. Hell, most years I barely took off work.

Today, my wife has been in the kitchen since dawn with a spreadsheet, an entire rope of garlic, and a Bing Crosby marathon on the stereo. Petey and I have been vacuuming and setting out extra chairs, since Alice's whole family is walking over in addition to my brothers and their growing families.

"Is dere juice, Daddy?" Petey looks out at me from under the dining room table.

"We have a whole case of juice boxes, kiddo," I tell him. "Want to help me get them from the garage?" He nods and we walk to the kitchen door, which is frosted over. It's been incredibly cold for November, even though Thanksgiving comes late this year. "Better grab a coat before we head out there, Petey," I tell him, holding out the bright red fleece that apparently used to be mine when I was little. My grandma found a box of kid clothes squirreled away in the attic when we renovated. My mom had bought really nice stuff, intending it to last through three kids. I smile thinking how pleased she'd be to know that her grandson is learning to work a zipper in the same coat.

I look over at Alice, sweating in a tank top with her hair tied on top of her head. Her Stag tattoo has healed by now, standing out fierce and black on her shoulder blade against her creamy skin. I still think it looks sexy as hell. She catches me staring and smiles. I cough, adjusting my pants, remembering that our son is waiting for me to grab the juice, and any minute now, our house will be filled with very loud, very opinionated relatives.

As if I conjured them, they start pouring in just as Petey and I get back inside with the juice boxes. The Petersons—Alice's extended family—all live a few blocks away, and they showed up en masse. Amy grabs an apron and starts helping Alice make side dishes while Amy's kids fight over who gets to baste the turkey first.

I'm about to yell at them when the front door opens and I see that it's Emma's friend Nicole. "Hey," I tell her as she strides inside like she owns the place. "I didn't know you were coming."

"I knew," Alice yells from inside the oven, and Nicole rolls her eyes. She thrusts a bottle of wine into my hands.

"I work all the time and my family is too uptight," she says. "Emma says I could horn in on some Stag madness without anyone getting judgmental."

I chuckle at the thought of my family in the position to judge anyone else. "You'll be trading a lack of judgment for everyone getting up in your business," I tell her. "This bunch never knows how to butt out."

Nicole laughs and pulls up a stool at the bar. Within a few minutes, she's giving Amy suggestions on how to do her nursing charts more efficiently and talking to Amy's husband Doug about grading his students' papers. While she solves everyone else's problems, an epiphany washes over me.

Suddenly the solution to my problems is plain as day, as if the "Star of Wonder" Bing is crooning about is shining down on my kitchen. "Nicole." I stand up and walk over next to her. "You have to come work at Stag Law."

Amy and Alice laugh, but Nicole simply cocks her head to the side and contemplates what I'm saying. "You know I have a career already, right Stag?"

I wave this away with a hand. "I'll pay you more and give you more creative control," I tell her. "I need a business manager. A process engineer. Someone to steer my firm, make strategic decisions while I handle the clients." It's the perfect solution I've been looking for. I don't need another lawyer. I can shake my wallet at the law schools up and down Forbes Avenue and find 50 good lawyers. I need someone with a mind for strategy, a cool decision maker. "I've seen you arguing Emma through a decision."

The words come before I pause to consider that this is a sore subject. Emma and Thatcher aren't even here yet, though. Fuck it. "Every time I see you, you're solving people's problems for them, or guiding them to make a more efficient choice. I need you. Stag Law needs you. Name your price, Nicole. You can start Monday."

I'm not sure what I expect from her in response to this outburst, but she swigs her wine and looks around the room. My nephews are clinging to my legs trying to avoid one another in a game of tag. I'd usually shake them off and shout, but I'm so sure of my footing today I just let them be. Nicole furrows her brow and says, "You're insane, Tim Stag. You know that, right?"

"I'm aware. I also know my client list is unbeatable. I've got a roster of hot clients a mile long. Plus, Alice makes all the food at work. Haven't I heard Emma say you sometimes forget to eat or have to send out your assistant while you work the treadmill desk?"

Within a few minutes, Nicole has negotiated an impressive salary and arranged to bring her assistant along with her to Stag Law. What the fuck do I care if she brings her own admin with her? I could never function without Donna. Nicole's guy will fit in just fine.

I surprise myself by leaning in for a hug, taken aback by my own excitement at this solution, but she places a palm on my chest. "We are not hugging, Timber. I don't do that." We are spared any awkwardness when Thatcher arrives with my father and Emma, who looks a bit gray but seems to be in a better mood today.

"All right, it's ready," I hear Alice yell from the kitchen. I look over my shoulder to see she's lined up the feast on the counter, buffet style. For the first time in weeks, I feel starved. My head is clear now, and I can settle down to really enjoy a feast. I hadn't realized how heavily my career situation was weighing on me on top of everything else.

Ty and Juniper bustle in the door just as everyone is sitting down, and Alice gives me a nod.

"Hi everyone," I say, tapping my fork against my beer bottle to get their attention over all the chatter. "It's been a crazy couple of weeks. I wanted to thank Alice for pulling all of this together for us." I'm interrupted by my family whooping and banging on the table in thanks, which makes me grin despite myself. "Go ahead and roll your eyes all you want, but I want us to take a moment and each share something we are thankful for. You can tackle me later when we walk up to the park to play some football." I have to yell now above my brothers groaning and making threats about my throwing arm. "So anyway, I'd like to start by saying how much I'm going to miss working with Her Honor, Judge Juniper Jones, but I'm thankful that I managed to poach Nicole Kennedy to join me as Director of Strategy at Stag Law." I raise my glass to Nicole, who nods. My family applauds and Alice teases that now I can finally pull the peppermint stick out of my behind.

I elbow my brother Thatcher to my left, who looks like he wants to go next.

He coughs and looks at Emma, who nods. Thatcher swallows and fidgets with his napkin before grinning. "Emma and I are going to have a baby. So I'm pretty fucking thankful for that."

Chapter 14

Thatcher

Emma and I fall asleep before eight o'clock on Thanksgiving. We stayed up most of the previous night talking about her pregnancy. We read every word Dr. Khalsa sent us and looked up the high-risk obstetrician that Tim emailed me about. It wasn't until Emma saw me finishing up making a nightlight for Ty and Juniper that Emma started crying and saying she definitely wanted to have our baby.

I pulled her into my arms and pressed her face against my chest, forgetting the fragile gift I'd worked so hard to get just right. The nightlight fell to the floor beside me as I held tight to this woman who means so much to me. I haven't been able to think about anything else since we got the news that Emma was pregnant.

It felt like a knife to my guts when Juniper found out she's pregnant, too. As soon as he got over the shock, Ty has been happy as shit about the baby and telling everyone he encounters that his wife is carrying his offspring in her womb. Of course I'm happy for my brother, but his obvious joy about the pregnancy is hard to swallow when my girl is struggling so hard with our news.

I wanted to do something nice for my brother and Juniper, so I made them a nightlight. I remember Tim and Alice were up all the time with Petey when he was young. Babies don't know night from day. I want Ty and Juniper to have a soft glow so they don't trip and fall over Ty's big shoes or something stupid like that. Especially while they're carrying the little Stag. Seeing me work that glass, hearing me explain it to her, Emma told me she had a vision of me as a father, and that made her feel happy. Safe. Hopeful.

So now Emma is finally feeling brave enough to consider *us* taking this journey. She's taking this risk with me, for us. A baby. A small Emma-plus-

Thatcher. I feel a knot in my throat and work to swallow it as I look over at her sleeping beside me in the darkness of early morning. We are supposed to go holiday shopping with my family today. Alice has a whole plan about hitting up the Christmas market and then going ice skating...I don't even know if it's safe to take pregnant ladies ice skating.

We eventually get up and head to meet my brothers, adding on extra layers since we will be outside for a few hours. Emma looks cute as hell in double leggings, since she says she can't get her jeans on anymore. I love watching her pore over the trinkets at each of the booths in the market, listening to the Christmas music piped in over the loudspeaker. I see a bunch of kids in line to visit Santa, and I can't help but grin. Here I am with my family. My future.

Emma drags me over to look at some homemade yard signs. The craftsman at the booth explains he can etch any last name into his templates. "We've got 'Santa Stops for Smiths,' or maybe, 'Johnsons On The Nice List." I try not to roll my eyes at the cheesy snowman and reindeer images, but Emma is into it, tracing over the sample signs lovingly. She walks away abruptly, and I frown again, remembering that there is still some outstanding legal business with me and Emma.

I'm hit by an overwhelming desire to make Emma somehow MORE mine. Right now. I want her to feel like we can buy a Stag Family yard sign. Like she deserves the tattoo Juniper and Alice got. All morning, I feel restless.

We find Tim and Alice and Ty and Juniper somewhere around the wooden ornament booth. The weather is gorgeous. The sun has that bright white hue only a crisp winter morning can bring, and I love looking at Emma's red hair flowing out from her white knit hat. She and Alice decide they want hot cocoa, and we walk away from Ty right in the middle of his outrageous story about some sort of rabid raccoons in his neighborhood.

"Dude!" he shouts after me as Emma and I duck into line at the cocoa stand. "I wasn't done telling you about the crazy woman whose cat got caught in the raccoon trap!"

Tim is of course interested from a legal standpoint and starts asking all about who is taking responsibility for the traps and any potential damage inflicted by the theoretical rabid raccoons.

Emma takes a sip of her cocoa as I fish some bills out of my wallet and I grin seeing the whipped cream mustache left behind after her first gulp. I lean in to lick it off her lip as my brothers groan and tell us to get a room. All of this—my brother telling some ridiculous story, my other brother wanting to know the legal ramifications—this all feels so right.

Even them teasing us about public display of affection. Except something about the way they say it makes me upset again. I don't need to get a room with Emma. We live together. I built a loft for her. For us. But I'm not married to this woman, and for whatever reason, that starts mattering to me a whole lot.

"Hey," I say as we all walk toward a stand selling handcrafted spoons.

"No," Emma says. "You cannot have a sip of my cocoa. Get your own."

"Very funny, Chezz. I was going to say...well, I was going to say I want to be your in-case-of-emergency person. Did you update your papers yet?”

She sighs. “Not yet, Thatcher.” I’m not sure why I’m pressing on this, but for some reason, as I look at all the couples around me in love, shopping for gifts together for their families, I just can’t stand it that Emma isn’t my *official* family. She’s growing my damn baby, and I’m not allowed to ask her doctor stuff about it if something happens to her. All the recent worry catches up to me all at once and I feel manic. I glance up at the clock above Santa’s cottage and remember that we are downtown on a Friday morning. It’s just after nine a.m.

“Come with me,” I say, grabbing her arm and hanging a sharp left from the Christmas market. I start stalking toward the courthouse.

“What the hell, Thatcher,” Emma hisses, clomping along behind me in her clogs. My brothers bought bags of warm nuts and follow along, curious, munching and teasing me, but I have tunnel vision. A singular plan. We enter the lobby of the courthouse and a quick look around shows me what I’ve been looking for: the service window for marriage licenses.

"Emma Cheswick," I say, not pausing, not stopping, heading right toward the window. "I want to marry you. Right now. I need to be your husband."

She raises an eyebrow at me. "You've got to be kidding me, right?"

I hear Ty and Tim laughing in the background, and I don't care. I feel like the whole world is off kilter. "If I'm your husband, they have to tell me what's going on if you're unconscious," I whisper-yell. The couple in front of us skips away with their paperwork.

"Thatcher." Emma yanks her arm loose and puts her hands on her hips. Juniper and Ty are cramming nuts in their mouths, watching us like we're in a movie or some shit. I shake my head and lean over into the window. The clerk looks at me with wide eyes.

"I need a marriage license," I say. "How long does that take?"

"Thatcher Stag, I do not agree to marry you," Emma protests. "Not this way. Not like this. What the hell is wrong with you?"

"You want me to get on one knee?" I ask, forgetting for a minute that my family thinks we've been actually engaged for years. The clerk slides me a piece of paper and I kneel, the cold marble seeping through the thin material of my jeans and making me shiver a bit. "Emma Cheswick, I'd like you to marry me. Right now. Please."

"This is unbelievable," Emma says, yanking the piece of paper out of my hands. She drops it in the trash can and storms out of the building, Alice and Juniper trotting after her. *Shit,* I think as the icy realization of my mistake settles into my bones. I get up and walk over to a bench and scrub a hand through my beard.

"Do you think she'll be back," I ask my brothers, who are still standing in the lobby staring at me.

Ty laughs and sits next to me, the wooden bench groaning a bit under our combined weight. "I do not think that, dude," he says. "What the hell is wrong with you?"

Tim puts his hands on his hips and frowns, then exhales slowly through his nose. "I know what you need here," he says, plucking the marriage license paper from the top of the trash. "Other than a notary, I mean."

"I'm listening..."

"You need a *gesture* now, Thatcher. Because, brother, that was really fucking painful to watch." Ty laughs and butts in that he thought it was hilarious. I punch him in the shoulder and that shuts him up. Tim folds the license and puts it in his coat pocket. He claps a hand on my back and says, "You need Mom's ring."

Chapter 15

Ty

Juniper scheduled her swearing-in ceremony on an off day for the Fury, so sure enough the entire team came to the courthouse to watch. All those big hockey players crammed in the seats beside Juniper's rowing friends and my extended family makes for a tall crowd.

And we're noisy as hell, because Juniper is awesome. She might not have any blood relatives, but she sure has a huge chosen family in Pittsburgh rooting for her. I love her confidence as she walks in, looking sexy as fuck in her robe and high heels.

She's only a little bit pregnant, and already her tits look massive, which I definitely appreciate. I sort of zone out during the short ceremony, because I get distracted by how good she looks. I can't tell if pregnant women really do glow or if she's just so damn happy to be made a judge that she shines. Either way, she looks good. I squeeze her hand and stand beside her, knowing Tim is taking pictures and I'll get to look at that expression she's got any time I want.

Alice wanted to cater the party for Juniper afterward, but we all talked her into being a guest and enjoying herself. Juniper let her pick out the restaurant and the menu, and as soon as we wrap up official City photos, everyone starts to head over to the fancy place on Penn Ave where Alice rented the top-floor party room. For some reason, Juniper said it was ok not to have alcohol since she and Emma can't drink. Alice suggested we go booze-free, which is ridiculous because Alice usually loves beer at a party. I leave my brother Tim to explain that my teammates are looking at a dry morning while I follow Juniper to her chambers to change.

"Mmm," I say, planting a kiss on her neck. "I love that you have *chambers.*"

"Meet me in my *chambers*," she says, tugging on my tie and pulling me into the room, which is really just an office with extra chairs so Juniper can hear smaller cases. She closes the door behind me and turns the lock. I cock my eyebrow at her, wondering what she's doing.

And then my wife leans back on her desk, hikes up her robe, gives me a full-on Sharon-Stone-style leg cross, and I see that she wore absolutely nothing under that thing for her swearing in.

"Holy fuck, JJ." I can barely form words. My dick immediately perks up. I feel like I'm drawn by magnets, stepping forward and sliding my hands up my wife's long thighs. The silky material of her robe bunches up at her hips and I stand in between her legs, pressing into her heat.

The air in her chambers sizzles with both of our desire. "It's been so long, Ty," she moans, leaning back on her forearms. "I need you to fuck me before we go to that party."

All those nights on the road that seemed so glorious before Juniper, are just long and lonely now that I'd rather be back with her. Then when I am home, she's been barfing or exhausted. We haven't had sex in weeks.

Today, I want to lick and savor every inch of her. I sink to my knees and duck my head under the hem of her robe, planting kisses up and down each powerful thigh. She trembles beneath my touch, moaning my name and letting her head drop back.

Eventually, after I make her wait awhile, I make it to her pussy. I slide one finger inside her and lick her long and deep, planting the flat of my tongue where I know she needs it most. Juniper makes sputtering sounds on the desk, moving her keyboard out of the way with an elbow as she gets herself comfortable. "That's it, babe," I growl, keeping up a slow rhythm with my fingers. "Tell me what feels good."

"Everything, Ty," she breathes. "Please." Her breath comes in puffs as I work her with my tongue, lashing away at her like she's my last meal. And fuck. She might be my best meal, because she tastes amazing.

"I need you to come for me, JJ," I say, worried that I might lose it in my pants if she keeps this up. The sight of her splayed open like this, just for me in her prim and proper work outfit, has me thinking dirty, filthy thoughts. I sneak a pinky finger further back as I thrust my hand in and out of Juniper, teasing at her tight little ass. This makes her groan and I feel her orgasm building around me until she erupts in my mouth. I lick up every drop of her pleasure and then kiss my way up her body. She's firm and tight, the years of muscles and intense workouts carving out a body as ripped as my own. I love how we fit together. I slip the robe up and over her head and then she drops her arms around my neck, sucking and nipping at my shoulder while I worship her tits.

"Juniper," I gasp. "These are fucking phenomenal."

She hisses when I pull a nipple into my mouth. "It's so sensitive, Ty," she gasps. I catch a hint of displeasure in her voice and pull back. She seems to relax against me then, so I kiss her lips instead and let her unbuckle my suit pants. She gets the belt undone and the zipper barely down before she's got her fist around my dick and yanks me toward her. "I need you," she says. "Now. Hard."

"Yes, Your Honor," I joke, but when I ram into her, there's nothing funny about it. The front of my thighs bash against the wood corner of her massive desk and I know it'll leave a bruise later, but I don't give a shit. I can't stop now. Not when my wife is demanding I go harder, deeper, as she grabs hold of my hips. She's totally naked, spread out on her desk, while I pound into her so hard her tits shake with the effort. She doesn't need to ask me, I know what she likes. But god, I love to hear it.

"I could do this forever, Juniper," I say, meeting her eye. The dark pools of brown are almost gone, her pupils are so dilated with her lust. She puts her hands on my ass, settling into the hollow beneath my hips, and pulls me deeper.

"Now, Ty," she insists. "Right now. Come with me!"

And I do. God, I come so hard I can barely see, melting into her, gasping and shaking as the milky jets finally slow down. "Fuck, Juniper," I say, leaning my forehead against hers. "How the hell am I ever going to step in here again and not think about this."

Juniper kisses me on the tip of my nose and leans back, reaching for a box of tissues. "I certainly hope you remember this every time you come to my chambers," she says with a laugh. "The Honorable Juniper Jones insists upon it."

I love hearing her giggle, seeing how excited she is about this new career move. She hands me a tissue and mops herself up a bit, still perched on the edge of the desk. I'm still standing motionless in between her legs, and she gently pushes me back. "You better close up your britches, Ty. We have to go meet a whole bunch of people for soup and salad."

I shake my head and grin, wondering how I got so damn lucky. She gets dressed quickly and we walk to the restaurant hand in hand. The press has found out the Fury are here—some server probably tipped them off—and the restaurant is mobbed with photographers. The manager won't let anyone upstairs, but the photogs snap shots of Juniper and me as we make our way inside. I've got the collar popped on my wool coat and a scarf wrapped around my neck, but there's no hiding who I am, especially with my team leaning over the balcony upstairs and hollering my name, plus a bunch of insults about the lack of beer.

"Will the baby play hockey?" a reporter asks as Juniper unzips her coat to hand it to the hostess.

She grins and they take some pictures, but all I can think about is how I don't want to leave her—them, really—tonight. I'm sick of the press and the fame. It's not exciting anymore. It feels invasive. My celebration with my wife should feel private, not gossip fodder by the checkout line at the grocery store. We fly out to Seattle for a four-day series, and I won't be here to get JJ ice cream if she wants it or spray that lavender stuff she likes when she can't sleep. As much as I love these guys, the glory, the fame...chasing a puck around with a wooden stick seems to have lost its appeal.

Chapter 16
Tim

With all the madness of the holiday season and everyone getting pregnant or elected, I haven't had a chance to hang out with my brothers in awhile. My grandmother reminds me of this at breakfast when she tells me she's not going to buy us running socks this year, since it seems like we don't even go running together anymore.

"Gram, you're being ridiculous," I scold, but I frown trying to remember the last time we hit the reservoir together. It might have been before Halloween. I pull out my phone and text them both to see when Ty is next in town.

Gram rattles the newspaper at me and says, "Read the sports page before you ask those kinds of questions if you don't already know the answer, Timber Stag."

"You know that Donna is the one who keeps track of all those sorts of dates," I tell her. "I've been stressed out trying to onboard Nicole."

"Onboard. Pah." She snorts. Alice left for work early today to set up the gingerbread structure contest for the team at Stag Law. She said it's a *structure contest* since not everyone will want to build a house. She ordered matching aprons for everyone who signed up. I don't think anyone will bill a single dollar's worth of time today, but Alice insists it's good for morale and Nicole backed her up. She told me it's an investment today for productivity and loyalty later. This is why I need Nicole. I don't know how to think about that shit.

My phone chirps in my hand, and I see it's Thatcher.

> Ty home today. Emma told me.
> I guess my wife watches
> hockey now??

Three dotted lines appear from Ty, and I know he's seen my message, too. A few seconds later, he writes,

> Can run as soon as I bang
> Judge Juney. Nobody told me
> how horny and demanding
> pregnant women get!!!!!!

I chuckle, remembering Alice in late pregnancy, how she was insatiable. I start wondering if Thatcher and Emma are there yet, and then I realize I don't want to think about my brothers' sex lives. I tap out a reply.

> Meet at reservoir in 20 min.

All of us show up within a few minutes of each other, stretching our quads against the stone railing at the top of the steps, looking down on the frozen park below. The air smells like snow, unusual for early December. But not unheard of. "You look like shit, Thatcher," Ty says, leaning on him for balance as he tugs one ankle behind him.

"Well, things are pretty shitty at my house," he spits back, giving Ty a shove. "Emma still won't talk to me after the courthouse." Thatcher nods his chin in my direction. "Buddy the Elf over here gave me mom's engagement ring, but…"

"You have to create the mood," Ty says, bending over and sticking his ass in Thatcher's face as he stretches. I laugh at the two of them, puffing out my cheeks against the cold.

"Let's go, guys," I say, starting off at a slow pace. "Gram says she isn't going to buy us the good running socks for Christmas if we don't hang out together." Everyone agrees that this is a bullshit threat. She's been getting us matching socks every year since we can remember, starting when that was about all we could afford for Christmas. I float the idea of inviting our father to come run with us sometime, now that he seems to be doing better, healthwise. Thanksgiving was civil…cordial in fact. But ultimately we decide these runs are for the three of us. A ritual we began when we had nobody but ourselves, a way to communicate when the words wouldn't come. The catalyst to dealing with any shit we may have simmering.

And right now, that barely-contained disaster is Emma and Thatcher. More specifically, Thatcher. I can see that even if I have my work situation straightened out, my family still needs me...or someone...for guidance. Thatcher's a damn mess.

"The way I see it," I say, inching the pace faster. "You're acting like I did when Alice first got pregnant."

Ty starts jogging backward, showing off and facing us. "You know, Timbo, that sounds about right. Thatcher is freaking the fuck out and trying to be all controlling and shit."

Thatcher shakes his head and stops in his tracks. "*You* are the ones trying to get me to woo her into some big-ass plan," he spits out. "She's wanted this for ages, and I've been too stubborn to notice and now that I see what she wants, I just want to get us there as soon as possible. That's all."

Ty cocks an eyebrow at Thatcher. "You done spewing nonsense yet?" He starts jogging again. "Like Tim said at the courthouse, Emma needs a gesture."

I nod my agreement.

"I sold my fucking truck. I bought an SUV!" Thatcher pulls off his beanie and shakes out his long hair. Tucking the hat in his back pocket of his sweats, he speeds up ahead. Despite the frigid air searing my lungs, I manage to keep up with him.

"You have to make yourself vulnerable," I tell him. "And you should probably ask Nicole for advice at this point. God damn, that woman has good ideas," I say. "And you should know by now that Emma needs time to adjust after you act like a cranky, bossy old man." Thatcher grunts, but I know he knows I'm right. I think this will be fine. It's almost Christmas. Everyone gets sappy and forgiving at Christmas—at least that's what Alice tells me.

I notice Ty is lagging a bit and I shoot him a dirty look. "What the hell is *your* problem," I say. "I don't know if we have time for more than one Stag Brother to be in crisis at a time."

Ty shakes his head. We run for a while longer in silence until Thatcher complains that his toes are going to snap off in the cold. We all walk back down to my house, passing my father-in-law out in the yard on the way. "Lights are looking good, Bob," I shout. "Love the lawn Santa."

Bob snorts and flips the bird at the generator behind the giant inflatable. "Amy's boys wanted this thing. Makes a damn racket."

"You could always cut it and tell them a squirrel chewed the cord," Ty offers, and we all laugh.

I drape an arm around his shoulder and tell him, "You're going to be a great dad, Tyrion."

Rather than crack a joke, he looks me straight in the eye. "That means a lot coming from you, Tim. Thank you."

Chapter 17

Thatcher

I'll give her a gesture, I think. I rummage through my closet to try to find a necktie. I haven't worn one since Ty's wedding. Hell, I don't even wear a tie when I have an art opening. Those shows are all about me anyway. Fuck anyone who tells me what to wear. But this morning isn't about me. It's about Emma and I need to make every effort to do this right.

I find the tie from Ty's wedding. I frown, noticing that it doesn't really match the pants I picked out, and, soon enough, I find myself wearing the entire rig I put on for my brother's ceremony. We all bought gray suits to match our eyes. I actually dig how I look in this vest and decide I'm going to start wearing these more often. The tie can go to hell, though.

I sigh and climb in my fancy family car, that I hope like hell will soon carry my family. Emma still hasn't told her parents about the baby, and through my entire drive to her father's office, I remind myself of this fact. "Don't mention the baby. Don't mention the baby." It becomes a mantra as I sit through tunnel traffic, and again as I wait for security to run my ID.

I grin at the receptionist who calls up to the senator's office to see if he will take an unannounced visit from his not-quite-son-in-law. The guy at reception is young and clean cut, looking much more comfortable in his suit than I do. He frowns, noticing the ink peeking out the edges of my cuffs, staring at my long hair. Fuck him. He finally hangs up the phone and sighs. "The senator says you should come on up, and grab yourself a complimentary coffee if you wish."

"Did he tell you that, or did he ask you to get the coffee for me," I ask. The guy rolls his eyes at me. "I like it black," I shout after him, making my way into Emma's dad's office.

"Stag," he says, rising and walking around the desk to shake my hand. We have a civil relationship, if not friendly. He leans back on the desk and crosses his arms. "I wasn't expecting to see you until Christmas Day."

"Nice to see you, too, Ed," I say, sitting down. And then I sigh. I didn't come here to be snarky with him. "I'll cut right to the chase."

"I'm listening," he says, arms folded, still leaning on the desk, and now towering over me. This fucking sucks.

"I'd like to marry your daughter, sir." I sigh.

He looks at me confused, and says, "I was under the impression you were already planning to do that."

I chew on the inside of my lip and lean back in my chair. "It's true. But I didn't speak to you about it, and I don't like that," I tell him. He opens his mouth to talk and I hold up my hand. "I don't think I need your permission. That's not why I'm here. Emma's a strong-willed woman and she'll do whatever the hell she feels like regardless."

He smiles at that. "She sure will, won't she." He walks around to his side of the desk and sits. "Well. So. You've been taking your time about marrying her, I'd say."

I nod. I exhale through my nose and lean forward. "I'm worried I missed my window."

He rubs a hand over his chin and frowns deeper. "I'll admit that I don't talk to her much about these sorts of things," he says. "But I've seen how she looks at you, Stag. And I've seen how you look at her. I don't think that look is going anywhere."

I tap my fingers on the edge of his desk before responding. "Things have been...complicated with us lately. My brothers are all—you know my sister-in-law is a judge now." He nods. "They're having a baby. My other brother hired a new strategy director or something."

"Well," Ed says, pointing toward the lobby, where one of my larger installations is displayed. "I think you're doing all right for yourself, too, Stag. You know I don't really know anything about art, per se, but your name shows up all over this damn city." He laughs. "I've promised your work more than once as an incentive. Your work is a hot commodity, it would seem."

This is probably the closest Emma's father will come to telling me he approves of me, so I decide to run with it. "I need Emma to know I'm serious about us. About her. About family. All of it. I thought maybe if I came to you, she'd see that."

The admin comes in with my coffee and plunks it on the desk so it sloshes a bit. "Jared," Ed barks. "The next time my son-in-law shows up, you get him his coffee faster. And you knock before you come in this office, young man." The kid turns red and shuffles out. I want to feel bad for him, but I'm clinging now to the hope that Emma's family can help me win back her heart.

"So tell me what's really going on," Ed says. "Emma's been thriving since she's been with you, much as it pains me to admit. She's healthy. She's working hard. I know she won that prize. And I also know something else is up, because she hasn't come to see her mother in a month."

I sip my coffee and think about how to proceed. I decide to tell him about the seizure, that it rattled her, and how I tried to drag her to the courthouse. This makes him straight up laugh out loud. "But, Ed, what do I do now? What comes next?"

He keeps on laughing and leans back in his chair. "Her mother proposed to me, you know. Not even a proposal, really. She told me it'd been long enough and we should get married already." Ed looks out the window. "I'm afraid I can't be much help to you figuring out how to untangle this mess, Stag." He meets my eye then and says, "But I will say I'm rooting for you to figure it out."

Chapter 18

Ty

"Damn, babe, did you see that? Did you see my game?" I greet Juniper with a kiss in the hall outside the players' lounge after my shower and media interviews. I was on fire this afternoon in our game against Toronto. "I slammed that Canuck into the boards. He barely knew what hit him."

"Yes, husband," she soothes, playfully. "You're strong as an ox. I'm going to need you to take your pregnant wife out for some food now, though."

We head over to Tim's place for Sunday dinner, only a few hours late. "I hope Alice saved us something," I mutter as we walk to the car. Used to be, my whole family would come to watch my games in person. That was back when Tim and Alice were secretly screwing in the executive lounge and Thatcher was sleeping around with… well he wasn't too particular now that I think about it.

Juniper squeezes my arm. "They come to plenty of your games, Tyrion. Don't be a pouter." Today was my last game before our break for Christmas. I was relieved to see we get four days off in a row. Juniper was able to shift around her midwife appointments so I can go with her tomorrow. We're probably going to get to hear the heartbeat, and I'm a lying fool if I pretend that's not the most exciting thing to ever happen to me.

When we roll into Tim's block, I see how the house looks all lit up in the early darkness of December afternoons. "Oh, Ty, it's like a storybook," Juniper says. I have to admit, Tim did a bang-up job hanging those twinkly lights. We didn't really get a good look at Thanksgiving when it was light outside. It takes me back to when we were young kids, and we used to always decorate. I catch a whiff of the pine boughs Alice hung from the windows and remember my mother, laughing, leaning out the window and asking me if I thought the greens looked okay. The force of the memory washes over me and I pull Juniper in close, spreading my hand across her stomach. I want my baby to know joy like that.

There's so much love and warmth in the house again I almost forget how gray it felt to live there in my teens. It was absolutely dreary here for a long-ass time. No fucking wonder I joined the NHL and didn't come back home for years.

I lean in and kiss Juniper, inhaling the scent of her. Sometimes I remember that she's mine to keep, and I get excited all over again. I feel pretty damn lucky as I walk in with her, arm around her shoulders.

Everyone else is done eating and spread throughout the downstairs. I notice Emma isn't here, and one look at Thatcher tells me not to bring it up. "Is he drunk," Juniper asks, settling onto a bar stool while Alice hands us plates of food she set aside.

"His eyes are glassy and he's staring into the fire silently, so I'd guess yes," I tell her, nodding hello at Tim while he and Petey assemble an electric train under their Christmas tree. "Holy shit, Timber! Is that ours from before?"

"Watch your mouth, Tyrion Stag," Gram yells from her rocker by the fire. She's taking pictures of Tim and Petey while they assemble the tracks. "And of course it's your train from before. I kept all that old stuff."

"We didn't get it out last year because Petey was still putting everything in his mouth," Alice explains. "But you know better now, don't you, angel?"

He nods. I sit on the floor next to them in delight, helping snap everything in place. Tim looks very serious when he hands Petey a beat-up old engineer hat and shows him how to work the train controls. "This isn't a toy, young man," he says, sternly.

"Of course it's a toy, Tim." I punch his arm. "Petey, dude, it's a toy train. Don't listen to him."

"Ty, please don't undermine me when I'm trying to tell my son he cannot crash his trains into each other, or into his toy cars."

Tim and I dive into a heated argument about the fun of running over toy action figures while Petey manages to get the train going on his own. Juniper watches it all with a smile on her face, one hand on her stomach, and I want to float away thinking about how this will be us with our kid in such a short amount of time. Then Gram asks me about flying out to our next game in Vegas, and I feel an icy dread in my stomach. I have to leave in the evening on Christmas to get to our game on the twenty-sixth.

When Petey starts to yawn, Alice declares it's past his bedtime. I guess that's our cue to go home.

I look over at my brother, who still hasn't said anything. "Thatcher, you want a ride home?" As I help Juniper into her coat, she starts yawning, too, and Thatcher shakes his head. He still doesn't say a word. I sigh.

Alice scoops Petey up the stairs and Tim walks us to the door, shivering a bit in the drafty entryway. "See you two tomorrow night?"

Juniper smiles, her eyes twinkling in the glow of Tim's holiday lights. "We'll be over as soon as our appointment's done at the midwife center," she says. "We're going to hear the heartbeat!"

Tim pulls her in for a hug, and I love seeing how genuinely happy he is for her. For us. For our family. Tomorrow is Christmas Eve, and while I love actual presents, I can't shake the sense that all I really want is to be over here with all of them. Not just tomorrow, but every day. I definitely understand why Alice insisted on living walking-distance from her dad and siblings. I drop a final glance at Thatcher by the fire and send out all my hopes that he and Emma will work shit out tomorrow. Nobody should be in a fight on Christmas.

There's no traffic in the afternoon on Christmas Eve, as it turns out. Juniper and I find a parking spot right outside the Midwife Center for our appointment. I know Carol the midwife stayed late and penciled us in as a special favor, so I made sure to make a hefty donation to their fund for healthcare for low-income women, which probably goes a long way to explaining the smile Carol gives when she sees us.

Carol opens the door as we walk up, shivering a bit. "Looks like snow," she observes, and as we walk past, she dips a scooper into the bin of rock salt near the door, scattering some on the sidewalk out front. "Can't have our pregnant mamas slipping, now can we?"

We walk up the stairs to the exam room, and on the way, I stop and stare at the rows of photographs. Decades of women and their babies smile down along both sides of the stairwell, including my own mother and me, moments after I was born. I kiss my fingers and touch them to the glass covering the photo, following my wife up to the exam room while Carol asks Juniper about her symptoms and talks about her transition to her new role as a judge.

Juniper gets herself situated on the couch in Carol's office while Carol whips out a stethoscope, checking out JJ's heart rate and blood pressure and stuff. "Everything seems to be going well," Carol says, massaging her hands around Juniper's abdomen. Carol grins at me as I wring my hands. I know all this stuff is important, but I wish she'd get a move on with that doohickey that lets us hear the heartbeat. That's the only part I can really experience, the only connection I have to the baby at this point.

I'm jumping out of my skin wanting to hear that sound.

"I think maybe Dad is a little anxious to hear what's going on in there," Carol says, leaning over to grab her microphone thing. "Juniper, can you slide your pants down a bit and pull up your shirt? You should be far enough along today that we can hear Baby Stag's heartbeat with the Doppler."

And then, Carol grabs hold of *my* hand and wraps it around the wand. She squirts some goo on my wife and asks if I'd like to try to find the heartbeat. I shake my head, terrified, and Carol says, "You aren't going to hurt a thing. I promise. Here." She guides my hand toward Juniper's stomach, and together, we press the wand against her taut skin. Juniper smiles as we start to hear the swirling static from the machine, and then—there it is.

"Aha!" Carol says, as Juniper blinks back tears. The static clicking sound makes way for thumps. An unmistakable, magical connection into the life my wife's body is building. Carol drapes her other arm around my shoulder as I start shaking, trying to hold back this wave of emotion washing over me. I don't want the sound to end, never want to break this connection with my child, but Carol turns off the machine, smiling, saying, "Heartbeat sounds just perfect. Perfectly healthy, like all the Stag babies I've seen." She cups my cheek. "Including you."

I feel so grounded right now, here with my family and this woman who literally caught me as I came into this world. I tune her out as she putters around, talking about Juniper's hormones. I lock eyes with my wife, not bothering to wipe away my own tears that fell while we listened to our baby's heart. "JJ," I whisper. "I'm going to retire from hockey. I want to stay home with our baby."

Chapter 19

Tim

"What time are they all coming again," I ask Alice from the dining room table as she flies through the house. She's been a little off lately, nervous and on edge. I keep telling her to relax, that this is just like any other family party we host every week. "It's like…" I look at my watch. "Babe, it's eight a.m."

Alice has her arms full of wrapped gifts she stacks by family unit. I see a six-pack of our favorite hazy beer from Grist House on the coffee table and curse under my breath that her brothers get the good stuff since I never remember to drive out there and buy my own.

"I'm just excited," she says, but her eyes don't quite seem joyful. After she arranges all the gifts, then rearranges them, she flicks on the stereo and blasts a Christmas mix from the radio. She and Petey start dancing as he crashes his trains into his toy cars. I grit my teeth and curse my brother Ty under my breath.

"Hey, Alice." I pat the chair next to me. "Come sit with me for a minute?" She shakes her curls over one shoulder and sighs. She bites her lips and walks over. As she plunks onto the seat next to me, I run my fingers through her hair and inhale the citrus-sweet smell of her. I plant a kiss on her cheek and say, "I want to give you your present early."

She shakes her head. "No way, Tim Stag. What am I going to open tomorrow morning?"

I laugh, but lean over to get the box I have sitting on the floor by the wall. "Don't worry about that, Mrs. Stag. But I want you to open this before you get too deep into your kitchen operation for today."

She cocks her eyebrow at me suspiciously and begins to tear open the wrapping paper. Petey runs over, wanting to help, and Alice grins as she lets him. Then she sees the label on the box and squeals, jumping out of her seat and clapping her hands. "Oh! Timmy! Yes!!"

I bought her one of those electric pressure cookers. The woman at the store said they're very popular right now and even "real" chefs like my Alice would appreciate them. I'm thrilled to see she was right. "Tim! It can do so many things. I wanted one so bad. How did you know?"

I pull Petey up on my lap and he laughs, watching his mother dance around with her kitchen gadget. "I'm going to make yogurt for the kids for tonight," she says. "Ooh, or should I use it for oatmeal for tomorrow morning? Oh! I wonder if I can pull off both..."

She sets it on the counter and sits on the floor with the instruction manual. I lean back in my seat, watching my wife enjoy herself, feeling like king of the world. I see my phone out of the corner of my eye and notice a text from Nicole. A glance shows me the thumbs-up icon, and I chuckle. In the few weeks she's been at Stag Law, Nicole has written a strategic plan for the next five months, five years, and five decades.

She's got systems for everything and has been talking to me about something called human-centered design and how she wants to apply it to our law practice. I pretty much do what she tells me in between sinking my teeth into big clients I suddenly have more time to prepare to meet. I spent this entire month fostering relationships with people I've been unable to touch base with for a long time.

Alice shakes me out of my reverie when she squeals. I look over and see a plume of steam escaping from the pressure cooker. "Petey, you must never touch this, okay" she quips. "Look! I'm manually releasing the pressure from my practice run!" We joke about the page she shows from the manual, sternly advising us to never put our face over the steam release.

"Good thing your sister Amy specializes in burn care," I say, pecking her on the cheek. "I'm going to walk over and see if your dad needs any help with anything." Bob recently moved into the third-floor apartment Amy and her family had been inhabiting, deciding the big downstairs portion of the house was too big for him alone, and Amy's three sons needed more space to spread out. I find that I like going over there and talking with him as I help him move his books and heavy things up the flights of stairs. It's nice having a father figure to bounce ideas off, talk about parenting. Bob would like me to care more about baseball than I actually do, but we've got years to figure it out. I love that he's not going anywhere. That this world I worked so hard to create feels so stable.

"Morning, Tim," Bob shouts as I round the corner, puffing out my frozen breath in the crisp winter air. "Looks like snow." He's salting the walk as a precaution, pointing to the horizon where a set of gray clouds rolls in. I make a note to check on the guest beds at home. If it does snow later, I don't want Ty and Thatcher driving home with their pregnant wives. No sense putting anyone at risk. Given our family history with car accidents, I know they'll listen to me and stay put to be safe if I ask them.

"Amy and the kids going to Doug's parents tomorrow?" I ask, helping Bob load a bunch of presents into a tote bag to carry over to my house. He nods. Both Alice's brothers moved out, and I know it weighs on Bob a bit that they left the neighborhood, even if they did stay in the city. "You know you're welcome over to our house tomorrow morning as well as tonight," I reassure him. Nobody should be all alone on Christmas day. "You can shoot the shit with my father," I remind him. "Talk about how the neighborhood's gone downhill since your day." He grins. He understands that things are complicated with Ted Stag, but I know Bob appreciates that we're including him in our celebrations. That's important to all of us, Stags and Petersons alike. Family sticks together.

As we walk home, I wonder if Alice did make yogurt with her pressure cooker, and I smile, planning to spend Christmas Eve drizzling lemon yogurt down my wife's chest and licking it off her. I cough, remembering that I'm standing next to her father. When we get inside, the house looks ready for a storybook party, but Alice is standing in the kitchen weeping.

"Pumpkin!" Bob rushes over to her and grabs her hand. "What's wrong?" Alice quickly wipes her eyes and looks up at me. She smiles, too quickly, and pats her father on the shoulder. "I was just missing Mom for a minute," she says. I frown as Alice rushes upstairs to change before my family comes crashing in. While I don't doubt that Alice misses her mother at

Christmastime, I can tell something else is going on.

Before I get a chance to follow her and see if she will tell me what's up, my family arrives and Christmas chaos ensues.

Chapter 20

Thatcher

I wake up on the sofa again, groaning when my stiff neck resists me turning my head. But then I see Emma standing over me, holding out a steaming mug of coffee. "Can we talk," she asks.

I bolt upright, shooting out an arm to drape over her shoulders, and remember that we've been fighting. I draw my arm back and nod, sinking back onto the sofa. She starts to cry. "I'm sorry, Thatcher."

"Hey." I risk putting an arm around her, and I sigh in relief when she lets me. "Em, I'm right here. And you have nothing to be sorry about."

"What are we going to do?" she asks, and I think about the past few weeks, making sure I enter this conversation in the right place.

"Why don't you tell me what you need," I say, and she looks over at me, wide-eyed. I pull her in closer to me, loving that she's letting me give her some affection. We've been distant and cordial, but haven't really had any big talks. Emma has had a few appointments with her medical team—it's been hell trying to schedule the neurologist along with the high-risk OB—but once we had our big meeting, they both reassured her that things seem very stable. She's not even risky enough to stay with the high-risk OB, which gave me a lot of relief even if Emma said she wanted to stick with the higher level of care. Just for reassurance, she said, and I admit I feel safer knowing we have a baby expert on our team.

I don't know how to help Emma feel less frightened about growing our baby, but I keep looking on that app to see what size fruit our little Stag compares to, and reminding her that her body has magically produced bones and organs and skin. Emma ditched wearing jeans a few weeks ago when they got too tight, and I wish like hell she'd let me run my hands over her growing stomach.

But I know that will come. I just need to be patient.

After I decided to tell her dad about my courthouse stunt, he pulled out a bottle of whisky from his desk and we got drunk in his office, talking about how poorly the Cheswick women handle uncertainty.

He'd said, "Emma likes to plan everything," and I told him how I foolishly tried to rush into a plan so everything would be tidy, taken care of.

"Hey, Ems," I say, tucking her red hair back over one shoulder and running it through my fingers. "Remember that time you helped me babysit Petey?" She nods and smiles as I recall his epic diaper blowout, and how we'd had to call Poison Control when he somehow managed to eat some diaper cream in all the mayhem. "You stayed so calm while all that was going on," I say. "I loved that about you. Even before I really knew that I loved you, I loved how you took action and did what had to be done."

Her eyes dance back and forth as she listens to my words. I tell her, "You know that you'll be an amazing mother, right? What you don't know, you'll research the hell out of until you do." I kiss the tip of her nose. Her breathing is ragged.

"I just...this isn't how I envisioned my life," she says, holding up her hands and gesturing around our apartment. "I mean, maybe this is. I don't even know what's going on in my head, Thatcher."

I hold out my fingers. "Let's see," I say. "You've got a hot fiancé." I grin. "You've got a ferocious best friend, an amazing job, an award-winning feature series." I open my palm and drop it to her belly, feeling a tingle through my core as I wrap my hand around the firm little bump. "And you've got your health under control, Emma. With people helping you keep it that way." She nods, letting me rub her stomach, explore the life blossoming inside of it. "You know," I tell her. "The Royal Baby will be born before ours, so you don't even have to worry that you'll pick some lame name that matches some duchess." She laughs, and I know I've got her with me, even if it's just for a minute. Even if it's just for right now.

"Maybe I want the baby to have a lame name," she jokes. "Maybe I want to name it Prince. Prince Stag."

"I was thinking more like Duke Stag," I counter. We share a laugh for a few minutes and she curls toward me.

"I'm sorry I've been such a bitch," she says. I kiss the top of her head.

"That's not what you've been," I assure her. "I came on way too strong at the courthouse," I tell her, remembering how Tim basically did the same thing when Alice got pregnant. Tried to drag her up to his penthouse and plan everything out without consulting her. I think about the plan I had in place to try again to get Emma to marry me. I'd had this whole elaborate scheme to ask her in front of my family at Tim's house tonight, make a public display of my devotion to her. But that suddenly doesn't feel right, either.

I've got the box with my mother's ring on top of the dresser in my room, but I don't want to break contact with Emma to go get it, scared the moment will slip away if I leave this couch for an instant. "Chezz," I whisper, twirling her hair around my finger again, nervous.

"Hmm," she grunts, seeming to almost drift off in peaceful sleep now that we've chipped through the top layer of our baggage.

"I still want all those things I was muttering about that day at the market," I tell her. "I still very much want to be your in-case-of-emergency person."

"Thatcher, I changed the paper—"

I cut her off with a finger to her lips. "Let me finish. I want to be your partner. I want to make a life with you, no matter what. I want to figure out communication skills together and learn how to manage my temper with you and maybe even figure out *your* temper someday…"

I shift my weight around, pivoting my arm out from behind her shoulders so I can kneel on the floor between her legs. She inhales sharply and meets my eyes. "Emma Cheswick," I say. "Will you marry me? For real and forever and preferably as soon as you feel comfortable?"

She giggles a bit and nods. "Not good enough, Chezz. I need you to say it. Please?"

"Yes," she laughs. "I will marry you." And then I kiss her, softly and deeply, trying to tell her all the words of my heart through my connection with her body. She groans and puts her hands on her stomach. "I guess it'll have to be soon if I want to wear the dress I got."

"What are you talking about?"

She stands up from the couch and walks down the hall to our room. I follow her as she starts chattering about how Nicole took her to the mall for maternity pants, but Emma got too overwhelmed to buy any and was feeling like a jerk for shutting me out when everyone knew we were going to eventually work it all out and get "actually married."

"Babe, you're rambling," I say, sitting on the edge of the bed. She rolls her eyes at me and opens the closet.

"As we were leaving, I saw this dress." She pulls out a pale-green dress. It's frothy and layered, with some iridescent bits that catch the light and look like rainbows. "It reminds me of...you know, the sculpture you made." I smile, remembering my Emma sculpture I'd made after I saw her standing in the sunlight once.

"A goddess," I say. "Rising from the sea."

She nods and gestures toward the dress. "I thought maybe I could wear this when we get married."

I jump up from the bed and grab the ring box. I kneel in front of her again, holding it up. "Ems," I tell her. "This belonged to my mother."

She gasps, pulling out the emerald-cut sapphire set sideways in a platinum band. "It's very important to my family, Emma, and so are you." I pause to take a breath, overcome by the weight of what I'm asking her. "My brothers both decided they'd very much like for you to have it," I tell her, "If you'd do me the honor."

Tears start to creep down her cheeks as she lifts the ring from the box. "Oh, Thatcher," she says, sliding it on her hand. I had it sized based on another one of her rings when Tim gave it to me the other week, so it fits her perfectly as she stares down at it. She whispers, "I'd be a real Stag."

"You're already a real Stag," I tell her, standing up and pulling her into my chest. "You've been a Stag ever since you wouldn't make out with me at the botanical gardens. You just didn't know it yet." I grin at her and she folds herself into my arms. "Come on," I urge her. "Let's go eat Christmas food with my brothers and you can show everyone your ring."

Emma starts peeling off her leggings and shakes her head. She grabs hold of my belt and says, "Before we do that, you need to help me work up an appetite." And then time stands still for a few hours.

Chapter 21

Tim

"We're here," Ty hollers as he kicks open the front door to my house, startling all the kids into silence for a moment. They'd been wrestling on the rug, making me nervous about knocking down the Christmas tree, so even though I want to be annoyed with Ty, I'm grateful he at least got the rascals to sit still.

"We can see that, Ty," I tell him, shaking my head as he takes off Juniper's coat and hangs it on the hook above the radiator.

He practically skips into the living room, though, looking like he's about to burst with some sort of news. "Out with it," I tell him. "What have you got for us?"

He plunks down a stack of gifts on the end table and Juniper rubs his arm. "We heard the baby's heartbeat today," she says. "And we got my bloodwork back."

Alice claps her hands. "That's so exciting! Which bloodwork was this?"

Juniper dances over to Alice. "The bloodwork that tells me this little Stag is a BOY!"

I grin and jump up, clapping my brother on the back and then looking down at the four little boys sprawled on the rug already. Next Christmas will be brutal. There will be at least six kids here. I make a mental note not to let Alice get any glass ornaments for the tree. "Dude, JJ," Ty bellows. "That's not even the exciting part." He touches my arm. "She's leaving out the exciting part."

I lift one eyebrow and look at them. Juniper smiles at Ty and nods, and he says, "I'm retiring from hockey. I'm going to be a stay-at-home dad with this little dude. Isn't that awesome?"

The room is silent. My grandmother's jaw drops. My father stands from his seat in the armchair near the fire. All I can think about is the work I went through to secure Ty's contract when nobody else in the NHL would sign him since he was such a hothead. "You're quitting hockey?"

He nods. He opens his mouth to start speaking, when the front door flies open again.

Thatcher and Emma burst into the entryway. I grit my teeth. With those two, you never know if they're going to be screaming or fucking behind my curtains. Based on the look on Emma's face, they took care of that second part recently. Thatcher dusts some snow out of her hair and kisses her on the cheek. "Were you all standing around waiting for us?" he asks, confused.

I shake my head no. The room is still silent as we wait for Ty to finish what he was going to say, but I notice Emma is dressed to the nines while the rest of us are sitting around in candy-cane pajama pants and reindeer sweaters—Gram's idea of a Stag family holiday uniform. "Good," Thatcher says, cutting me off before I can talk. "Because we need Juniper to notarize our marriage certificate and then marry us."

There's a long moment where nobody says a word, and then Ty starts laughing sort of maniacally. "Good one, Thatch. Heh heh. So anyway, back to me retiring…"

"I'm not kidding," Thatcher says. He lifts up Emma's hand, and I see she's wearing Mom's ring. "Emma is on board to marry me. And she wants to do it while she can still fit in her amazing fucking dress, because if you hadn't noticed she's growing my baby. Our baby."

He puts one hand on her stomach and Emma smiles shyly. Everyone looks back and forth between Ty and Thatcher and their pregnant wives. Then Gram starts cackling. "What the hell is in the water that's got you boys losing your damn minds?"

"Gram, did you just do a swear?" One of Alice's nephews is stuffing popcorn in his mouth, watching while all the adults come unhinged. Everyone titters, realizing the magnitude of Gram using a curse word. And then they all look to me, waiting for direction on how to proceed I guess.

I clear my throat. "Okay, so, maybe we should all sit down and talk about all of this? Ty and Juniper, you were here first, so you can begin."

And then instead of passing out gifts, my brothers tell us about their plans, that turn out to be not so hasty after all. Ty has been feeling misplaced for a long time, sore after games and practices, and badly missing his family. "I could barely get to the hospital when Emma had that seizure," he says. "Ems, I'm real sorry I blurted that news to you like that."

"No harm done, Ty," she says, her arms crossed over her bump. I smile, seeing the round protrusion. She's not very tall, short like Alice, so I know it won't be long before she blooms into a fully pregnant-looking person. I wonder if she and Thatcher know the sex of their baby yet...and then I remember that we are mid-trial, with my brothers each outlining their major life events.

Ty continues, explaining how he had an epiphany while listening to the baby's heartbeat and doesn't want to miss a single minute, not for hockey, which he calls "just a dumb-ass game in the end. Besides," he says. "Even if we make the playoffs, JJ isn't due until late June. This guy will stay in there until I'm back to take care of him while Mommy goes out and dispenses justice and shit."

Juniper rolls her eyes at this. "Ty, come on," she squeezes his hand. "You can't swear like that around our son." I try very hard not to bring up Ty's contract with the Fury. This isn't about work tonight. This is Christmas Eve and we are supposed to be gathered here to celebrate family. Juniper looks over at Emma and Thatcher and asks, "Care to tell us how you two made peace with one another?"

Before Ty can crack a sex joke, Thatcher dives into his side of the story, talking about how Emma is going to be able to take things easy while she works on her book, which should give her a lot of flexibility in case her pregnancy and her epilepsy get dicey. "And you all know I don't do anything but sit around and play with glass all day," he says. "Seriously, though, it sounds like Ty can just watch our kid along with his and we don't need to worry about daycare."

Emma tells us a bit more about how she eventually calmed down and stopped being angry with Thatcher for dragging her into the courthouse so hastily. I scratch my chin and wonder if everyone is just drunk on eggnog or if there really is something to the idea of the Christmas spirit driving people to make rash choices. I must be caught up in it all, too, because soon enough, a Christmas wedding sounds like a fine idea.

"Hey," I interject. "Emma, would you like me to call Nicole? I mean, if you're going to get married right now. Do you want her to be here?"

"Oh!" she claps her hands. "That's such a great idea. I guess I should call my family, too. They probably won't come. They're at the country club Christmas dinner..."

I've already texted Nicole by the time Emma's done talking and received back a string of profanity, followed by an emoji of a lightning bolt and a car. I look over at Thatcher, who is grinning like a fool, and ask him if he plans to get married in his Christmas pajamas or if he wants to borrow a suit. "Fuck no, I don't want a suit," he says. "Sorry, Gram. But when do I ever wear a suit?"

"Apparently you wore one to go talk to my dad," Emma teases, hanging up the phone. Her mother's hysterical shrieks echo through the room as Emma slides her phone into a pocket in her dress. "My parents are on their way. Alice,

Tim, thank you so much for letting us barge in your house with my family."

"Barge? Are you kidding?" Alice is crying again, wearing an apron, and frantically whisking a bunch of things at the kitchen island. "This is amazing. It's fine. It's all fine. I'm going to make a wedding cake in my new pressure cooker!"

My family looks at me wide-eyed, and I chew the insides of my cheeks, remembering Alice crying earlier. I suggest that they all break into groups to make wedding arrangements while I see what Alice needs.

When I walk into the kitchen, she's leaning over the pressure cooker, which keeps beeping as she struggles to fit on the lid. "Damn it," she swears, slapping the device. "Come on!"

"Babe," I walk up behind her, placing my hands on top of hers. "Can I help?" She shakes her head, curls sticking to her tear-soaked cheeks. "Is there a recipe I can read over with you, Al? Or maybe you can let me help you with the lid for this thing?"

Alice throws the heavy lid down on the kitchen floor and I step back so it won't land on my toes.

"Hey," I try to soothe her. Her nostrils flare out and I place my hands on her shoulders. "We are a team, Alice Stag. Now tell me what's going on."

She puffs out her breath, blowing a few curls out of her eyes. "I'm pregnant, that's what."

I feel my heart actually stop beating for a moment and wonder if I maybe heard her incorrectly. "Come again?"

"I said I'm pregnant. And now they're all going to think I did it on purpose to steal their thunder and this was going to be your Christmas news tomorrow morning because I just don't want to take away from anyone else—"

"ALICE!" I place a finger on her lips for a minute. "Baby, let me have a second." I breathe slowly in and then out again, remembering how it felt to become a father. Remembering, too, how it felt to have my world ripped into chaos and uncertainty, and how that all turned out to be so fulfilling in the end. "I thought I had everything figured out," I said, looking up as Nicole bursts into the house and storms over to Emma. "And really, I have nothing figured out." Alice starts to cry again. But I continue, saying, "That's so fantastic, Alice."

I pull her into my arms, enveloping her in my body. I start kissing her head, rubbing my hands up and down her back. "Are you really happy about it," she asks, her voice muffled in my sweater.

"I'm terrified! And overjoyed! I feel so many things at once, Alice."

She sighs. "Me, too," I hear. And we bend down together to pick up the lid so I can help her finish making a wedding cake.

Chapter 22
Thatcher

I can't believe I finally get to marry Emma. It feels like we've done absolutely everything backward. Pretending to be engaged when we barely knew each other. Getting pregnant. Hauling her into the courthouse. But this? As we stand around Tim and Alice's backyard, this feels absolutely perfect. A light snow falls as Ty lights tiki torches around the perimeter of the yard. Alice's brothers brought over some leftover strands of twinkle lights from the Peterson house and sort of draped them over the apple tree, so everything looks really pretty.

Nicole is inside fixing Emma's hair and finding her a warm wrap to wear with her dress while I work on getting Amy's sons to stop digging holes in the yard, where Emma will walk up to meet me at the makeshift archway we made from a bunch of old hockey sticks and some zip ties. Ty, smirking, hangs a sprig of mistletoe from the middle of the arch and claps me on the back. "Let's get this moving. I'm freezing my nuts off out here."

He jogs inside and shouts for everyone to come out in the backyard, and Emma's mother and sister bustle out, chirping about how unconventional all of this is and wondering how they will ever look their country-club friends in the eye again. My father helps my grandmother into a lawn chair near the archway and walks over to me. "Thatcher," he says, setting a hand on my shoulder. I don't flinch or brush him aside, which feels like progress. "I want to thank you for letting me be here to see you married," he says and bites back a sob. I realize I'm the only Stag brother who will have a parent present at his wedding, and that makes me choke up a bit, too.

All I can do is nod at him, but I'm seized by a strong emotion looking up at the mistletoe and I grab his arm. "Will you stand up here? With me and Ty and Tim?"

His mouth works up and down like he's searching for words, and he nods, standing behind me, but not too close to the precarious archway. It feels right to have him there, like this new chapter of all of our lives, all these changes, circle back to include him, too. Family looks and feels so different than I ever thought, and today it all feels welcome for the first time I can remember.

Amy and Doug, holding up a set of speakers from inside, start playing some music from Doug's phone and everyone quiets down. This is what I've been waiting for—my chance to seal my commitment to Emma. To *our* family.

Juniper walks out the back door toward the arch, wearing a flowing black robe and carrying a few sheets of paper. "Where did you get a judge robe?" I ask her, wide-eyed.

Tim and Ty take their place beside me and Tim winks. "It's my graduation gown from law school," he says. "Close enough."

I don't hear anything else, then, because I look up and Emma is walking toward me, her arm linked with her father's. Nicole has her phone out, taking a thousand pictures as my Emma glides through the yard. I think about how different I am from when I met her a few years ago. How much I work to be a better person, to be honest with my family, and make myself vulnerable to Emma.

"All rise for the honorable Judge Juniper Jones," Ty shouts, crushing the mood.

"Knock it off, Tyrion," Tim says in his sternest dad-voice.

Juniper clears her throat and says, "Well, thank you all for hanging out back here with us in the snow and freezing cold. I've never actually performed a wedding yet, so this is exciting for me." She flashes a huge smile at me as Emma shivers a bit from where she's facing me. Juniper looks at Ed and says, "I think you can hand her off to Thatcher now, Senator," and she gives him a wink that makes him laugh. He pats Emma on the hand and steps back with her mom and sister.

I reach for Emma and see she's carrying a bouquet of poinsettias she must have gotten from in the house somewhere. I love how the red petals play off the red and gold highlights in her hair, the green of her dress. It's all I can do not to run off and immortalize this moment in my glass studio. But I need to focus, to be here. Present with my family this Christmas Eve, where I'm receiving so much more than I could ever wish for.

Juniper keeps talking, saying, "The bride and groom were pretty clear that they don't want a drawn-out ceremony. Their engagement lasted long enough. So anyway, really the only required parts are that you each agree to marry one another and then I can do some declaring...but do you want to say anything? Vows off the cuff?"

Emma nods. She's a writer. I should have expected that she'd have something magnificent to say, but I'm unprepared to hear her start telling me, "Thatcher Stag, you started out as such a cad. But I then saw through the chinks in your inked-up armor, and boy. Do I like what I found in there." She dabs at her eyes. "When you open your heart up to me, when you tell me all the things that frighten and inspire you, all the things that bring you joy...I want to be with you. I want to be the arms that hug you, the whispering voice of reassurance, the nagging wife who begs you to get your hair cut so I can see your beautiful grey eyes." She reaches out and strokes my cheek gently. "I know I'm not very good at staying calm or dealing with my fear when I don't feel in control, especially about my health. But I know that you're here for me, to keep me safe and to make sure I get all the help I need from the people who know how to give it. I'm so excited to make a life with you, Thatcher, as your friend and your partner and your wife."

I lean in to kiss her but she tilts her head back. Juniper whispers that I'm not supposed to do that until I've at least verbally agreed to marry Emma. "Well," I say, "It's really hard to follow that. All I know is that you're brilliant, Emma. I mean that in every sense of the word. There is a brilliance that shines from you and it inspires me. I told you, you're my muse. I want to live up to your light so I don't seem dim beside you. You make me better, stronger, and a more complete person. I was wading around in a sea of bad choices before I met you, and you reached down and pulled me into this lifeboat. You'll make me the luckiest man around if you let me be your husband, Emma Cheswick. I love you with every cell of my body, and I love even more that you're so bravely growing this new life for us." I have to stop then because I'm about to cry and I feel a knot in my throat that chokes me. I let the tears flow, because fuck it. If a man can't cry at his own wedding, well...fuck it. "I just love you, Emma. And I know I mess up a lot, but as soon as I realized I wanted to spend the rest of my life with you, I wanted that to get started. Right away. You're the best gift I ever got, and I'm so excited to get out of the snow and take you home as my wife this Christmas."

And then I don't wait for Juniper, but I lean in and kiss my girl. I pull her close against me, letting my lips meld with hers, until we feel like one being. Emma pulls back with a slight gasp and drops her hands to her belly. "Mr. Stag," she says, beaming, "I just felt Prince Duke kick!"

"My kid has much better timing than me," I say, dropping a hand to her belly, wanting him to know I'm right here and I'm not going anywhere.

Juniper declares us husband and wife and my family erupts into cheers. I lean in again and kiss the hell out of Emma until Ty rips down the mistletoe and starts shaking it in my face. Emma laughs and shakes her shoulders. Her teeth start to chatter and I kiss her once more. "Come on," I tell her, yanking her toward the house. "Let's go inside, Mrs. Stag. Alice made cake."

Epilogue: Ty

Six Months Later

Someone throws me a water bottle after the final buzzer sounds. Game seven of the Cup final, here in Pittsburgh, and we won two-nothing. I know I've won a cup before, and I've played thousands of hockey games in my career, but knowing this is the last one, I'm real worked up. Everything seems to slow down as I look around the arena. I hear the roar of the crowd, see my teammates clapping each other on the back. My coach comes out and pulls me in for a hug, saying, "I'm really gonna miss you around here, Stag."

"Thanks for giving me a chance, Coach," I say, clapping him on the back.

"Sure you won't change your mind about this?" I shake my head then, and he sighs, walking away to the crowd of ecstatic fans.

I know I should take off my helmet and talk to the press, but I want to keep it on for just one more minute, savor these last seconds as a pro hockey player. The guys in suits come out on the ice, rolling out the little carpet they put down so nobody drops the Cup. There's a squad of guys wearing special white gloves and they present the cup to our captain, who immediately skates over and hands it to me. Me!

I'm the first one to get to do my victory lap hoisting the Cup. I toss off my helmet then and make my way around the rink. I pause beneath the box, where my family is pressed against the glass, going wild. Thatcher is up front, holding their tiny baby, Wesley. He came a little earlier than they were expecting, but Wes and Emma are both doing great. Well enough to come to a nighttime hockey game, anyway. I shake the cup in their direction, and see Tim gesturing for Juniper to come down.

He sure as hell better help her get down here. At 38 weeks pregnant, she's still rowing every day on the rowing machine, so she's no slouch. Even if I do have to hand her the handles, since she can't reach around that Stag-baby belly. But I can't have my pregnant wife slipping on the ice. Then I remember that Alice is pregnant, and Tim probably won't want to leave her alone up there. He gets extra nuts about safety when Alice is pregnant. We've been teasing the hell out of him, getting all anxious again right after he started to calm down. I frown, wondering who is going to give JJ a hand, and then I see my father helping my wife down the stairs. That makes me smile. I'm glad he's here with us this time to see me win the Cup. Mom would like that. Ted should be around for all these moments. Hugging all these Little Stags.

I finish out my lap and hand the cup off to the next guy, staring around the arena at all the fans, who are waving flags and pumping their fists as they shake their Fury jerseys, many of them with my name on the back. I never thought anything would top this feeling—being part of the best team in pro hockey. But this doesn't even compare to how I feel when I see my pregnant wife smiling at me from the entrance to the ice.

I know the team is going to ask me to say something about my retirement, and I make my way over to help her out to the podium before they hand me the microphone and ask me to comment about my choice to quit hockey at 29 when I've never even had a major injury.

I pull my wife in closer and she doesn't even wince at the smell of me in my gear or my sweaty jersey. The reporter makes his way over to us, asks rapid-fire questions, and hands me the mic. "Look," I say. "Hockey has given me so much. When I was a young kid in trouble, hockey gave me an outlet for my anger and my grief. Hockey brought me home to my family and let me experience teamwork." I give JJ a squeeze. "But this woman right here? She's growing my *son*. And this is my whole world right now. There's nothing more important to me than being here for them." I drop a kiss on Juniper's cheek, thinking about how proud I felt when she won Olympic gold, but how hard it was for me to get away to be there for her when she hit that milestone. I don't want to repeat the mistakes of our father; I don't want to miss one difficult or one joyful moment of this family life. "I want to make Team Stag my priority, and I truly hope my fans can appreciate how much that means to me."

Juniper starts to shuffle off the ice with me, but I'm still in my skates, so I bend down and scoop her up to thunderous applause from the crowd. She nuzzles her nose into my neck and says, "I thought you were going to talk about your long-term plans to coach at-risk kids?"

I shrug, setting her down on safe, dry ground. "There's time for that later," I tell her.

I look ahead down the hall and see security escorting my family down to greet me. My entire family—my father, my grandmother. Both my brothers. Their babies. Everyone in the world who matters to me is right here, together. I pull everyone in for a group hug, and smile. The Stag family is cranky and loud and up in each other's business, and every bit of it feels perfect. Together, we have come so far. And right now? The Stag family is exactly where we need to be.

* * *

Thank you SO MUCH for following along with the Stag brothers. But...there's another Stag brother...

Beautiful Game is the story of Hawk Moyer, secret Stag! Turn the page for a sneak peek.

If you want to see Nicole get her happily ever after, you can look for her in Foundation: A Grouchy Geek Romance.

Large Print Titles By Lainey Davis

Stag Brothers Series

Sweet Distraction (Tim and Alice)

Filled Potential (Ty and Juniper)

Fragile Illusion (Thatcher and Emma)

A Stag Family Christmas

Beautiful Game (Hawk and Lucy)

Stag Generations Series

Forging Passion (Wes and Cara prequel)

Forging Glory (Wes and Cara)

Forging Legacy (coming soon)

Forging Chaos (coming soon)

Bonus Epilogue: Thatcher

Two Years Later

"Babe, did you pack my phone charger?" Emma is a task master getting ready for this trip. It's our first time leaving Wes overnight with all his cousins at Ty and Juniper's place, and Emma is transforming her anxiety into checklists. After Emma's book released, she's been invited to talk all over the place. She either brings Wes with her or only agrees to video chat in for lectures about writing and human rights and all that stuff Emma gets pumped up about.

This time, the whole Stag family staged an intervention when she got invited to give a lecture at Oak Creek College. We can drive there in a day, stay a few days at one of those bed and breakfast places chicks love, and maybe conceive Stag Baby #2 if I have anything to say about it.

I give my studio one final look over to make sure all the fires are out, and then walk back upstairs to help keep Wes out of Emma's way while she freaks out. I find her sitting on the floor in Wes's room surrounded by pajamas. Wes stands behind her pulling her hair and jabbering about his cousin Odin. I kneel down and put my hand on Emma's leg. "Chezz," I say. "Can I help?"

She shakes her head. "I don't know how many pajamas he will need and I just think maybe it's too soon and what if it snows?"

I open up the duffel bag and toss in two pairs of pajamas. "Babe, it's three nights. He'll be with Uncle Ty and Odin, and I'm sure they'll hang out with Petey and Byron. It's going to be a party." I lean across her lap and shove a bunch of pull-ups in the bag, too. "Besides, if he wrecks his clothes, he's the same size as all the other Stag kids. Nobody will let Wesley be cold."

"Odin!" Wes starts clapping and I scoop him up. I look at my watch and tell Emma, "Ty's gonna be here in his Dad Mobile any minute. You ready for this?" She shakes her head, and I help her to her feet. Emma reads me the rest of the checklist and we watch as Wes puts his sweatshirt on backwards, then refuses to let Emma fix it.

I hear Ty fucking honking his horn outside, like he's the pizza guy or some shit, but I sigh keep my red words to myself so Wes won't repeat them. "Emma, you going to come down and make sure he's got the car seat right?"

Ty dove into this stay-home dad business head first. He's like the toddler whisperer, and he took all sorts of car seat classes and baby CPR. I know damn well Emma trusts him more than me with Wes in the car. But I also know she's not about to skip a prolonged goodbye.

When we get outside, Ty slides open the door to his minivan and I see he's got both of Tim's kids in there, with Wes's seat set up next to Odin. "Wanted to make sure they could punch each other properly," Ty says as Emma buckles Wes in. The two boys immediately start pulling each other's hair and I have a powerful memory of fighting with my brothers in the back seat of our parents' car.

"How come you have Timber's rugrats," I say, ruffling Petey's hair.

"Dude," Ty says, slipping in some kid tunes playlist. "More kids is less kids. They occupy each other. We're having a party." Ty looks over his shoulder and then stage whispers to me, "Alice begged me to take them this afternoon so she and Tim could bone."

Emma bursts out laughing at this and then blushes, because we're about to go upstairs and do the same thing. I toss the duffel bag up front and Ty gives us both a salute. As soon as he pulls away, I slip a hand onto my wife's ass for a proper squeeze. "Come on, Chezz," I whisper into her ear. "Let's get a head start on our vacation plans."

We arrive in Oak Creek a little later than we intended. I had forgotten how much I love just talking to Emma about all the things she thinks are interesting. Every few hours, she'd say something about researching pepper jelly or alternative fuels, and I'd have to pull over and fondle her awhile. I hope this place we're staying in has thick walls. I intend to get loud.

Turns out, there's not much to the town of Oak Creek. The college is set back across the creek from the town, which radiates out from a circular street around the library. Our B&B address just said Main Street, so Emma tells me to pull over in the first spot I find and she wants to get out and walk.

"Is that a Houseplant Hospital?" She asks, tugging me across the street. There's a lightness to her now that we've arrived. I know some part of her mind is getting ready to give a talk about her book, but the rest of her is truly enjoying this quirky ass place full of random people doing Tai Chi in their yards like it's not 4pm on a weekday.

"Chezz, what the hell is this place?"

"Oak Creek is a small college. They've got a pretty strong science program, but are really strong in creative programs, too. That's why they want me to come talk to their students!" Emma runs her hands along one of those Little Free Library boxes. This one's shaped like an oak tree and I grunt, admitting that's pretty clever.

"Hey, Ems, do you have a quarter in your purse? The meters here take actual quarters." I haven't seen a real parking meter without a card reader in...I don't really leave the city much and when I do it's for the woods. I don't think I've been anywhere with a mercantile, let alone a Main Street.

We drift around the town center and don't find the inn, but Emma starts yanking on my arm. "They have a *Thatcher Park,*" she squeals. She runs toward the little parklet, tugging me behind her, and I take a minute to nod my head at the beautiful glass street lamps. "It's like Narnia," Emma whispers, touching the lamp post and picking her way gently along the path. We step past a bench and I see a bright blue Victorian building. I don't have to look at it twice to know that's our destination.

I can absolutely tell that whoever runs this place is going to be *very* talkative, and I flare my nostrils, trying to breathe deeply and remember that I at least get my wife all to myself to sleep tonight. The inn has solar panels clinging to its sloped roof and a huge garden of wildflowers out front. A bunch of butterflies take off as we walk closer, and the front door bursts open.

"Ohh!" A woman claps her hands together and smiles at us. "You must be the Stags! I'm Indigo, owner of the Oak Creek Inn. It's painted indigo. Get it?"

Emma smiles widely at Indigo and rushes up the steps to pump her hand. "Would you believe that my husband's name is Thatcher? Just like your park?"

Indigo squeals and she and Emma jump up and down on the porch like they've known each

other their whole lives. "You're just going to love it here in Oak Creek," she says. "Come on in and I'll tell you all about it."

* * *

Want to learn more about this place?
Check out my Oak Creek series,
a set of small-town steamy rom-coms.
Coming to large print in 2024

www.ingramcontent.com/pod-product-compliance
Lightning Source LLC
Chambersburg PA
CBHW010350170726
48285CB00010B/2762